Fragments of Fear

Seven Tales of Darkness and Dread

R. Rivera

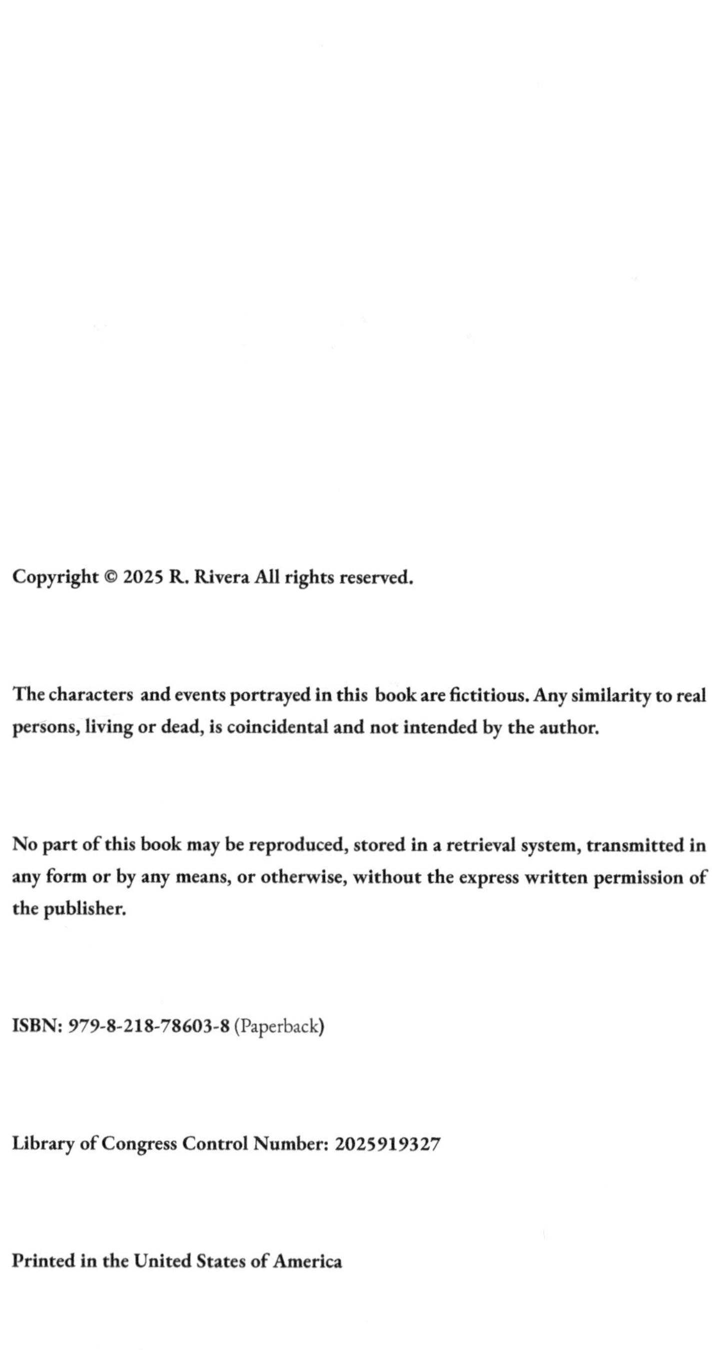

ISBN: 979-8-218-78603-8 (Paperback)

Library of Congress Control Number: 2025919327

Printed in the United States of America

For the past me, the kid with too many stories in his head and not enough pages to hold them. And for the writers who showed me the way—Stephen King, R.L. Stine, and so many others who proved that words can frighten, haunt, and inspire. This is where those dreams finally found a home.

"We make up horrors to help us cope with the real ones."

Stephen King

Preface

I have always loved stories. Some kids wanted to be athletes or astronauts. I just wanted to read. I can still remember being a kid and discovering the Goosebumps series by R.L. Stine. Those books cracked the door open for me, showing me that horror could be fun, addictive, and scary in all the right ways. They were my first taste of the shadows.

Later, I found Stephen King. And that was not just cracking the door open. It was blowing the whole thing off its hinges. The very first book of his I ever read was *The Shining*. I found it in my high school library, sitting quietly on the shelf, waiting for me. I checked it out not knowing that it would change the way I saw storytelling forever. That book showed me that horror could be more than just scares. It could be unsettling, heartbreaking, and deeply human. It introduced me to the kind of suspense that crawls under your skin and stays there, and it taught me the power of psychological depth. I fell in love with the idea that the scariest monsters might not be outside at all, but inside the human mind.

That sense of tension and unease shaped the way I started to see stories. I became fascinated with what drives people to act the way they do. Alongside King, my other influences came from television. I was hooked on shows like *Criminal Minds*, *Law and Order: Criminal Intent*, and *Law and Order: SVU*. Those shows gave me a window into darker corners of human behavior. They were not about monsters in closets or ghosts in the attic. They were about people, their secrets, and the terrifying things they were capable of. That blend of crime, psychology, and suspense fed directly into how I would one day shape my own stories.

There was also something else I carried with me from the books and shows I loved. I was always drawn to a good twist ending. The kind of ending that makes you sit back, re-think everything you just read or watched, and feel that shock in your chest. I admired the writers who could pull the rug out from under me in those final moments. When I began writing my own stories, I knew I wanted to do the same. A story without a twist, for me, always felt unfinished.

Like a lot of writers, I started with a big dream. I had the vision for a novel, start to finish. The problem was the middle. That stretch of road where the story slows down and you are not sure how to keep pushing forward. I would write a little, then take long breaks. Write some more, then take longer breaks. Eventually, that first project got shelved.

But I was not ready to give up. Writing was still in me, and the itch never went away. So I turned to short stories. They kept me sharp, kept me practicing, and most importantly, they kept me falling in love with writing again. What you are holding now, *Fragments of Fear*, is the result of those moments.

These stories are not perfect. They were never meant to be. They are pieces of imagination and fear, fragments of the kinds of tales that once kept me up at night when I was a kid, flashlight under the blanket, flipping through *Goosebumps* or the latest King novel. They are experiments, snapshots of characters in moments of dread, survival, and discovery. They also carry with them the fingerprints of every influence I have ever had: King's psychological depth, Stine's fun but frightening chills, the crime shows that explored the dark corners of humanity, and my own love for a shocking twist.

I hope at least one of them sticks with you. I hope at least one of them gets under your skin the way the best horror always does. Because fear is not just about monsters or shadows. It is about us, about the things we bury and the truths we avoid.

Thank you for picking this book up. Thank you for giving these fragments of fear a place to live, even if just for a few hours of your time. And if you are anything like me, the younger me who dreamed of doing this, maybe this book will remind you that stories are worth writing, even when they come out in fragments.

R. Rivera

Contents

Scars of the Storm

Chapter One

The Bookstore

The day was like any other for Megan. She steadily worked through a string of errands and a mental checklist. She thrived on a routine. It wasn't exciting, but it was comfortable.

As she drove through the familiar streets of her small town, something unfamiliar caught her eye. A brand-new sign stood at the edge of a strip mall, where an old laundromat had been: "Hidden Chapters Bookstore."

Megan's passion for books was profound, compelling her to spend more time on shelves than in front of a television. While major retailers had their appeal, they could not compare to the unique ambiance of a small, independent bookstore. Thus, she promptly turned into the parking lot, temporarily setting aside her errands.

The door jingled softly as she stepped inside. The air smelled like paper, wood, and the faintest hint of coffee. It was quiet, save for the muffled footsteps of a few other customers. Megan glanced around, taking in the rows of towering shelves packed tightly with books, their spines creating a kaleidoscope of colors.

She ran her fingers over the shelves as she walked, pausing occasionally to tilt a book out and read its cover. Each title seemed to whisper to her, offering its world for her to escape into. This was her happy place.

Turning a corner, she spotted a small display with a handwritten sign: Staff Picks. Her eyes scanned the selection until they landed on a title that stopped her cold: "Haunted Memories" by Roger Green.

Her friend Paul had told her about it when she went to get her computer checked at the computer shop where he worked. He told her it was a "must-read." Megan had made a mental note to pick it up eventually, but she had not expected to stumble upon it here. And it was on sale. She smiled, a small thrill of satisfaction spreading through her chest.

She picked up the paperback, running her thumb along the edges of the pages. The cover was striking—dark and foreboding, with an image of a foggy forest silhouetted by the outline of a shadowy figure. It was precisely the kind of story she loved: suspenseful, eerie, and unsettling enough to keep her on edge.

Megan tucked the book under her arm and wandered toward the counter. The cashier, a young woman with glasses perched on her nose, gave her a warm smile. "Good choice," she said, nodding toward the book. "Thanks," Megan replied. "I've heard good things about it."

As the cashier rang her up, Megan felt a quiet excitement bubble inside her. She loved the anticipation of starting a new book, of diving into a story where anything could happen.

When she stepped back outside, she noticed the shift in the air. The sky had darkened to a dusky gray, and the wind had picked up, swirling stray leaves around her feet. Megan paused for a moment, inhaling deeply. She loved storms—the smell of rain from an approaching storm, the sound of rain on her roof, the flashes of lightning, the distant roll of thunder—it all made her feel alive.

Sliding into her car, she set the book on the passenger seat and glanced at the thickening clouds. A storm was coming, and she could not wait to settle in for the night.

Chapter Two

The First Signs

When Megan pulled into her driveway, the sky had grown even darker. Heavy gray clouds churned above, and the air had that distinct, charged scent that always came before a storm. She paused momentarily in her car, listening to the faint patter of raindrops on the windshield. There was a quiet thrill in the anticipation—she had always loved storms.

Gathering her bags, Megan went up the front steps and into her cozy little house. It wasn't much, but it was hers. The walls were lined with bookshelves, each one crammed full. She had stacks of novels in almost every room, some in neat piles, others leaning haphazardly. It was the kind of clutter she loved—evidence of a life immersed in stories.

She dropped her keys on the counter and started unpacking her groceries, placing each item in its designated spot. The rain outside began to pick up, and a steady drumbeat on the metal roof echoed softly through the house. Megan glanced at the window, catching the faint shimmer of water running down the glass.

Her new book sat on the counter, its glossy cover gleaming under the kitchen light. She couldn't resist flipping through it as she put away the last of her groceries. The pages smelled fresh and slightly inky, which she always associated with new beginnings. She smiled, already imagining herself getting lost in its story.

After finishing her quick chores, she made a simple sandwich and poured a soda. She ate while standing at the counter, her gaze occasionally flickering toward the window as the storm grew louder. By the time she finished, she could hear faint rumbles of thunder rolling in the distance.

After her meal, Megan headed to her bedroom to change into comfortable clothes. She slipped into her favorite oversized T-shirt—a soft, well-worn one that hung loosely past her hips—and her go-to pair of slip-on shoes. As she caught her reflection in the mirror, she couldn't help but laugh softly. She looked utterly relaxed, the perfect outfit for a quiet evening at home.

Grabbing the book from the counter, Megan went to the living room and sank into her favorite rocking chair by the window. The chair was old, a gift from her grandmother, and its wooden frame creaked with every sway. The sound was soothing to Megan, a reminder of all the nights she'd spent here, book in hand, listening to the rain.

She settled in, tucking her legs under her and opening the book. The words on the page began to draw her in, but the storm outside quickly became a rival for her attention. The raindrops hitting the roof had grown louder and more insistent, and the occasional clap of thunder seemed to reverberate through the walls.

Megan glanced at her book, watching the wind tossing the trees outside. Their branches swayed violently, some bending so far they looked like they might snap. The storm was picking up faster than she'd expected, but instead of worry, she felt a quiet thrill. She had always found storms exciting.

Lightning flashed suddenly, lighting up the room for the briefest of moments. Megan smiled to herself and leaned back in her chair, the book resting on her lap. Tonight was shaping up to be exactly what she'd hoped for: the perfect storm and book.

Chapter Three

Howl of the Storm

The rain tapped steadily on the metal roof, a rhythmic lull that mingled with the creak of Megan's rocking chair. She shifted her weight slightly, letting the chair sway back and forth as she turned the page of Haunted Memories. The words on the page were captivating, pulling her into the eerie world of the book, but something outside kept tugging at the edge of her focus.

Glancing up from the book, Megan peered out the window. The rain had intensified, its soft patter steadily drumming against the glass. She could barely make out the outline of her garden through the thick veil of falling water. The wind gusted suddenly, sending the trees into frenzied motion. Their branches whipped back and forth, clawing at the sky like desperate hands.

Megan shivered though the house was warm. The storm had taken on an almost malevolent energy, making the air feel heavy and electric. She tightened the blanket draped over her lap, trying to shake off the faint unease creeping up her spine.

Lightning flashed, illuminating the room in a brilliant white light for the briefest moment. It was followed instantly by a deafening crack of thunder that rattled the windows. Megan jumped, her heart racing. She pressed a hand to her chest and exhaled sharply, laughing nervously at herself.

It's just a storm, she reminded herself. She had always loved storms, after all—their raw power, the chaos of the elements colliding. But tonight felt different. The rain grew heavier, hammering against the roof like a relentless drumbeat. Megan closed her book, unable to focus as the noise swallowed the room. She leaned forward in her chair, staring out the window. The wind howled like a wild animal, and the occasional metallic groan from the roof hinted that parts of it were not holding up well against the storm's fury.

A sudden clatter outside made her jump. She squinted into the dark, straining to see through the rain-streaked glass. The wind had picked up pieces of lawn furniture, tossing them across the yard like discarded toys. A garden chair slammed against the side of the house, the sound sharp and jarring.

Megan stood, her heart pounding, and moved closer to the window. She could feel the cold draft seeping through the glass's edges. Another flash of lightning illuminated the yard, and she caught sight of one of her roof panels flying away, tumbling into the chaos outside.

"Great," she muttered under her breath. Repairs were not what she wanted to deal with this week. As she turned back toward her chair, the sound of hail began to join the cacophony. At first, it was faint—a few scattered clicks against the metal roof. But it escalated into a barrage of sharp, relentless clinks and clanks within moments. The noise was deafening, drowning out even the howling wind.

The hail began to strike the windows, each impact a sharp, threatening crack. Megan froze, her eyes fixed on the glass. "Come on, hold together," she whispered," she was talking to the window or her fraying nerves.

The wind shrieked, pushing the hail harder against the glass. Each hit felt like a countdown to something inevitable. The house creaked and groaned, the storm testing its strength. And then it happened.

The window closest to her shattered with an earsplitting crash, sending shards of glass flying into the room. Megan instinctively raised her book before her face, a feeble shield against the onslaught. The sharp sound of the breaking glass and the icy gust of wind that followed knocked her off balance, and she stumbled back into her chair.

A sharp pain bloomed in her hand. She lowered the book and looked down in horror. Blood dripped from several deep cuts across her palm, but that wasn't the worst of it. A large shard of glass had embedded itself in the top of her hand, pinning it to the book. The paperback was slick with blood, the bright red stark against the dark cover.

Megan's breath came in shallow, ragged gasps as she stared at the grotesque sight. The pain was sharp and searing, but her shock dulled it enough to let her move. She tried to free her hand, but the glass wouldn't budge.

The wind tore through the shattered window, whipping her hair into her face and scattering shards of glass across the floor. The storm outside seemed alive, screaming its fury into her tiny house.

Megan clutched the book with her uninjured hand, her mind racing. She had to free herself. She couldn't stay here, not like this. But no matter how hard she tugged, the glass held firm. Blood trickled down her wrist, warm and sticky against her cold skin.

The storm raged on, relentless and uncaring. Megan was trapped by the chaos outside and the growing terror inside.

Chapter Four

The Storm's Fury

The pain in Megan's hand was unbearable. Blood poured freely from the gaping wound where the shard of glass had pierced her palm to the book. Her breathing came in short, shallow gasps as she sat frozen in her chair, staring at the grotesque sight. She tried to move her fingers, but the sharp edge of the glass cut deeper with every twitch.

A violent gust of wind tore through the shattered window, scattering debris across the room. The chilly air bit at her skin, making her shiver, but the storm outside felt almost secondary to the chaos in her mind. Panic was rising fast, threatening to drown her in its grip. She couldn't stay like this. She needed to act.

Megan reached for the embedded shard with her uninjured hand, her fingers trembling as they wrapped around the slippery, blood-coated glass. She took a deep breath and pulled. A sharp, searing pain shot through her hand, so intense that it brought tears to her eyes. She let out a strangled scream and released her grip, unable to continue. The glass remained stubbornly lodged in her flesh, unmoving despite her efforts.

"No, no, no," she muttered, her voice trembling. The wind howled louder, rattling the house like a beast trying to claw its way inside. The hail continued its relentless assault, slamming against the remaining windows and roof. Another loud crack echoed through the house as a piece of debris struck one of the walls.

Megan's mind raced. She needed a new plan. Gritting her teeth, she leaned forward, placing the book flat on the floor. Her blood smeared across the cover as she braced it with her foot, anchoring it in place.

"This has to work," she whispered, more to herself than anyone else. She closed her eyes and yanked her hand upward with all her strength.

The glass tore through her flesh with a sickening rip. Blood spattered across the floor as she stumbled backward, clutching her hand. The pain was overwhelming, but the shock dulled it just enough for her to look at her injury.

Her palm was ruined, a gaping hole where the glass had been. The edges of the wound were jagged and raw, blood pouring from the open flesh. Megan's stomach turned as she stared at the grotesque sight, her breath coming in short, panicked gasps.

She raised her hand, almost involuntarily, and peered through the hole. The sight felt surreal, like something out of a nightmare. She couldn't process it. Her mind struggled to catch up with the reality of what was happening.

But the storm wasn't done with her. A loud, metallic groan tore through the air, louder than any thunderclap. Megan's eyes darted toward the window, where the wind had begun tearing more pieces of the roof loose. She barely had time to react before another violent gust sent a large chunk of debris flying through the shattered window.

It happened so fast that she didn't even have time to scream. The jagged edge of the roofing material struck her neck with brutal force, severing her head cleanly from her body. Blood sprayed in a wide arc, staining the walls and floor in vivid red.

Megan's head hit the ground with a dull thud, rolling until it came to rest under the bed. Her lifeless eyes stared into the darkness, frozen in an expression of shock and horror.

Her body remained in the rocking chair, slumped slightly to one side but still upright. The chair swayed gently, its rhythmic creaking eerily unchanged despite the chaos around it. Blood dripped from the edges of the chair, pooling on the floor beneath it.

The storm continued its relentless assault, the wind screaming through the broken window as if mocking her lifeless form. The house groaned under the pressure, but inside, everything was still.

Chapter Five

Final Echoes

The storm's rage showed no sign of relenting as Megan's body sat lifeless in the rocking chair. The chair swayed gently back and forth, its rhythmic creaking eerily consistent, as though mocking the chaos that had unfolded just moments before. Outside, the wind continued to howl, tearing through the night with primal ferocity.

Rain poured through the shattered window, pooling on the floor and mixing with the blood that had spread in dark, glistening streaks. The once-cozy room was a scene of utter destruction—shards of glass were scattered across the floor, pieces of debris were strewn about, and the overturned furniture bore the marks of the storm's fury.

Under the bed, Megan's head lay motionless, her wide, lifeless eyes staring into the shadows. A thin trickle of blood ran down her cheek, pooling on the hardwood floor beneath her. The storm outside roared on, indifferent to the carnage it had left in its wake.

As the hours passed, the storm began to wane. The hail lessened, the deafening drumming against the roof fading into softer, intermittent taps. The wind no longer screamed but sighed, its once-violent gusts reduced to gentle whispers that slipped through the broken window. The house, which had been groaning and shaking under the storm's weight, now stood still, battered but intact.

In the aftermath, a haunting silence settled over the room. The rain had slowed to a steady drizzle, the occasional droplet still finding its way through the broken window and falling with a faint plunk onto the floor. The rocking chair continued its gentle creak, swaying back and forth, propelled by the residual energy of the storm—or perhaps something else.

The first light of dawn began to creep through the jagged opening where the window had once been. The faint, gray light illuminated the wreckage, casting long shadows across the bloodied floor. Megan's body sat slumped in the chair, her arms hanging limply at her sides.

The wound at her neck was jagged and raw, the edges already beginning to darken as her blood cooled.

Her head remained under the bed, its glassy eyes staring into the growing light. The faintest glint of the morning sun caught the surface of her pupils, giving them an unnatural shine that seemed almost alive. But Megan had no life left in her now.

The house was unnaturally still, save for the creaking of the chair and the faint drip of rainwater. Its silence felt heavy and oppressive as though the air held its breath.

Outside, the neighborhood stirred back to life. Birds began to chirp tentatively in the distance, their songs hesitant after the storm. Branches and debris littered the streets, evidence of the storm's fury. But inside the house, time seemed to have stopped.

The book Megan had so eagerly bought lay discarded on the floor, its cover stained with blood. The title, "Haunted Memories," seemed almost mocking now, as though it had foretold what was to come. The pages were warped and damp, the ink beginning to smudge.

Hours passed before the sun rose, casting brighter light into the ruined room. The rocking chair finally slowed, its creaking diminishing until it fell silent. The house grew colder, the broken window letting in the crisp morning air.

And then, as the first rays of sunlight struck the bloodied floor, the faintest sound broke the silence—a soft, almost imperceptible rustling. The book's pages fluttered slightly as if stirred by an unseen hand. The cover shifted ever so slightly, nearly as though it were breathing.

In the stillness, the house seemed to hold its breath, waiting for something. The shadows deepened, stretching across the room in unnatural patterns. Under the bed, Megan's lifeless eyes caught the faintest flicker of movement, and for a moment, it seemed as though they stared back.

Epilogue

Breaking News

"This just in—this week's unexpected storm left a trail of destruction across the region, knocking down several trees and power lines. Utility crews are working tirelessly to restore power to affected neighborhoods. Officials are urging residents to stay clear of downed lines and debris."

The screen shifted to images of streets littered with fallen branches, crushed mailboxes, and bent street signs. A mangled traffic light hung twisted, its metal casing dented from the storm's wrath.

The anchor's voice continued, the camera returning to his somber expression.

"Unfortunately, the aftermath of the storm also brought tragedy. Authorities have confirmed a fatal accident involving a vehicle and a pedestrian late last night. According to reports, the woman driving the car is in stable condition with minor injuries. However, the pedestrian was pronounced dead at the scene.

"At this time, no names have been released out of respect for the family's privacy. Details surrounding the accident remain under investigation, and no further information is available currently."

The screen switched to footage of emergency crews working after the storm. Red and blue lights reflected off the rain-soaked pavement as responders cordoned off a section of road. A single car sat with its hood crumpled, the windshield shattered. A tarp-covered form lay on the sidewalk nearby, a lone shoe peeking from under the edge.

The anchor's voice softened. "Our thoughts are with all those affected in the wake of this week's storm, particularly the victims' families. We'll update this story as more information becomes available."

Hello
Paul

Digital Hostage

Chapter One

The Drop Off

Sundays were Paul's least favorite day at the computer repair store. Not because it was hectic—it wasn't. It was the opposite. The hours dragged, and the only thing keeping him sane was the faint hope someone might come in with something interesting, like a hard drive packed with illegal files or some unhinged conspiracist's secret manifesto. But no, it was primarily mundane crap.

At 3:52 PM, eight minutes before he could finally lock up and go home, Paul was sweeping the floor, thinking about what sandwich he'd grab on the way back. Then it happened: the door chime. The sound made him freeze mid-sweep.

"Shit," he muttered, gritting his teeth. "Who the hell comes in now?" He saw a middle-aged man standing in the doorway, wearing a dull gray suit that seemed allergic to dry cleaning. The guy's face was pale and blank, as if he were waiting for someone to tell him how to emote. His eyes scanned the room slowly, making Paul uncomfortable.

"Uh... can I help you?" Paul said, trying to sound polite but annoyed.

The man didn't answer right away, which only made it worse. He shuffled to the counter and placed a battered laptop case on top with all the care of a man dropping off a ransom note.

"There's something wrong with it," the man said, his voice low and monotone.

Paul raised an eyebrow, already suspicious. "Okay... what seems to be the problem?"

The man stared at the laptop like it was some ancient artifact. "It's... acting strange. Programs keep opening on their own. Videos, files. I didn't put them there."

Paul sighed. "Sounds like malware. Or maybe porn pop-ups got you. You'd be surprised how many guys come in here with their laptops infected because they couldn't resist free 'local singles in their area.'"

The man didn't laugh. Didn't even blink. "Right," Paul muttered, pulling the laptop closer and opening the case. It smelled faintly of mildew and something metallic, like old coins. He popped open the lid of the computer, only to find it dead. No power cord, of course. Fucking typical.

"I'll need the charger," Paul said flatly.

"I don't have it," the man replied, glancing at his watch. "Can I just leave it here? I know you're about to close. I'll pick it up on Tuesday."

Paul hesitated. He didn't want to deal with this. But the guy had this weird, unsettling vibe, and Paul wasn't in the mood to argue. "Sure, just let me get your name," he said, turning to grab a customer form. That's when the door chime sounded again. Paul whipped his head around. "Sorry, we're closed!" he called out automatically.

There was no reply. He frowned, leaning to see past the man, but no one was there. When he turned back, the man was gone. The laptop remained on the counter like a ticking time bomb.

"What the actual fuck?" Paul muttered under his breath. He walked to the door and poked his head outside. The parking lot was empty. The man had vanished like a bad dream.

"Well, that's just fucking fantastic," Paul muttered. "You drop off your creepy-ass laptop and then just disappear like a goddamn magician. Great. Love that for me."

He thought about leaving it at the store, but something about the situation gnawed at him. It wasn't just the man's strange behavior—it was how the shop felt after he left, as the air had shifted as something had stayed behind.

"Alright, fine. I'll take you home," Paul said to the laptop as if it could answer. "But you better not be some cursed shit," he said to himself, half-joking but also half-serious. The stories he'd read online about haunted items constantly flooded back when stuff like this happened. It's probably just a cheap Dell with a virus, he thought. Still, something about it felt… off.

As he locked up the shop and headed to his car, he muttered to himself, "If this thing starts playing creepy music or flashing ghost shit on my screen, I swear to God, I'm throwing it in the fucking river." He didn't know it yet but regretted taking it home.

Chapter Two

In Their Sight

Paul kicked off his shoes as he entered his apartment, a laptop bag in one hand and a crumpled fast-food bag in the other. His place wasn't much—just a modest one-bedroom where he spent most nights eating takeout, fixing other people's tech, and occasionally binge-watching old sci-fi shows. Tonight wasn't going to be one of those peaceful nights.

He plopped the mysterious laptop onto his kitchen table and pulled out his food: a sandwich, some chips, and a soda. Before plugging the computer in, he leaned back, thinking about the drive home.

Paul pulled out of the computer repair shop's parking lot; he spotted Stacy sitting on a bench near the corner of the street. She was a familiar figure in the neighborhood—homeless but always polite and soft-spoken. Paul didn't know much about her, but he often saw her quietly keeping to herself near the park or outside the coffee shop.

Today, she was hunched over, sipping from a Styrofoam cup, her threadbare jacket doing little to protect her from the brisk chill. Her backpack sat beside her, patched and frayed from years of wear.

Paul slowed down as he passed, glancing at her in his rearview mirror. He'd spoken to her several times before, usually offering her a few dollars or a cup of coffee. She'd always accepted gratefully, her quiet "thank you" lingering with him long after.

A pang of empathy stirred in him. She probably hadn't eaten much today—if anything at all. Without giving it much more thought, Paul decided to grab her something. He drove a few blocks to a sandwich shop, the bright sign promising "The Best Sandwiches in Town."

As he walked inside, the warm smell of fresh bread and sizzling bacon greeted him. The shop was bustling with activity, a cheerful contrast to the cold streets outside.

"Hi there!" said the cashier, a young woman with a bright smile.

"Hey," Paul replied, stepping up to the counter. "I'll take two combos, please. One turkey and Swiss on wheat, and one ham and cheddar on sourdough."

"Chips and drinks come with those," she said. "What kind of drinks would you like?" "I'll go with a cola and water," Paul said. "Great! That'll be $18.50."

Paul handed over a twenty and stepped aside to wait. He glanced around the shop, enjoying the light chatter and upbeat music. A couple of kids were giggling at a corner table, and a barista was humming along to the tune on the radio.

A few minutes later, the cashier called, "Order for Paul!" "Thanks," he said, grabbing the neatly packed bags.

In his car, Paul returned to where he'd seen Stacy. She was still there, her eyes fixed on the ground, the Styrofoam cup cradled in her hands.

He pulled up slowly and rolled down the window. "Hey, Stacy!" he called out, his voice warm.

She looked up, startled for a moment before recognition dawned. A small smile softened her tired expression. "Hey, Paul."

"I brought you something," he said, stepping out of the car and handing her one of the bags. "Turkey and Swiss, chips, and water. Thought you might like a meal."

Her eyes widened, and she took the bag carefully as if it might slip through her fingers. "You didn't have to do that," she said, her voice soft but filled with gratitude.

"I know," Paul replied with a shrug. "I wanted to."

Stacy hugged the bag to her chest. "Thank you, Paul. This means a lot."

He nodded, giving her a small smile. "Take care of yourself, alright?"

"Yeah," she said, her lips curving into a faint smile. "You too, Paul."

As Paul drove away, he glanced at her in his rearview mirror, carefully unwrapping the sandwich. A quiet sense of fulfillment settled over him. Small gestures didn't change the world, but for someone like Stacy, they could make all the difference in a day.

He'd driven off after that, a tiny flicker of warmth in his chest. Helping Stacy always made him feel better about his otherwise uneventful life.

Now, as he sat at the table staring at the strange laptop, that warmth was replaced with a creeping unease.

"Alright, let's see what the hell is so special about you," he muttered to the laptop, grabbing a compatible charger from a tangled drawer of cables. After plugging it in, he powered it on and took a bite of his sandwich while it booted up.

The desktop was loaded. Everything looked surprisingly normal: the default wallpaper, a few scattered folders, nothing alarming at once. He relaxed a little.

"See? Just another shitty computer. Bet the guy was too cheap to get antivirus software," he said, washing down his sandwich with a sip of soda.

But then his eyes landed on a dead-center folder on the desktop. It was titled, in all caps: I DON'T WANT THESE FILES. Paul froze, a chip halfway to his mouth.

"Okay... that's not ominous at all," he muttered sarcastically. His curiosity quickly got the better of him. He clicked on the folder.

Inside were three files: 1.exe, 2.mp4, and 3.txt. He let out a laugh, more nervous than amused. "Oh, good. Numbered files. Super fucking original. What's next? A picture of a ghost?" Paul clicked on the executable file first. The screen flashed red.

"FUCK!" he yelled, nearly tipping his chair over as he jerked back. But before he could fully process what happened, the red screen disappeared, replaced by the standard desktop.

"What the...?" he muttered, staring at the screen like it might grow teeth and bite him. He tried to open the file again, but a pop-up message appeared: This program is already running.

He rubbed his temples. "Running where? Hell? My nightmares?" Still unsettled, he moved to the second file: a video labeled 2.mp4.

When it opened, Paul saw a man sitting in a dimly lit, windowless room with brick walls. He stared directly into the camera, his expression blank but his eyes sharp, almost predatory.

Paul felt his stomach knot. "Oh, shit. This is about to get weird, isn't it?" In the video, the man spoke in a low, calm voice.

"If you're watching this, whoever gave you this laptop, you just saved their life. But in doing so, you've put your own in grave danger. I can't explain everything here, but the text file will."

He paused, and for a moment, a faint smile crossed his lips. "God bless your soul."

The screen went black.

Paul sat frozen in his chair, the sandwich forgotten on the table. His hands were clammy, his heart pounding so hard he could feel it in his throat.

"What the fuck... what the fuck?" he whispered. He stared at the laptop like it was some cursed relic, which, at this point, it might as well have been.

He debated slamming the thing shut and throwing it in the dumpster, but the third file opened on its own before he could move.

Paul flinched, nearly falling out of his chair again. The text file was blank at first. Then, slowly, letters began appearing, one by one, as if being typed in real-time:

Hello, Paul. Enjoying that sandwich? Paul's stomach dropped. His eyes darted to the half-eaten sandwich on the table.

"Nope," he said aloud, pushing back from the table. "Nope. Nope. Nope." He slammed the laptop shut, breathing heavily. His phone buzzed on the counter, making him jump. He grabbed it, his fingers fumbling.

It was a text from an unknown number. The first one is free, and the second will cost you.

"What the fuck is going on?" Paul said, pacing the room. His phone buzzed again.

Open the laptop, Paul. Read the file. Trust me—you don't want to make this more complicated. Paul stared at the screen, his heart racing. Against his better judgment, he sat back down, flipped the laptop open, and stared at the text file. Words were appearing:

Good. Now that I have your attention, the real fun begins.

He swallowed hard, dread pooling in his chest.

Please don't fall asleep on me, Paul. It's going to be a long night. Now, finish your sandwich.

Paul's eyes darted to the webcam at the top of the screen. Without hesitation, he grabbed a roll of duct tape and slapped a strip over it. "How about that, you bunch of voyeuristic fucks?" he muttered. The laptop beeped.

What did I say about second chances, Paul? Time to pay the price.

A low hum filled the room, coming from outside. Paul froze.

Chapter Three

Terms of Survival

Paul gripped the table's edge, staring at the laptop like a ticking time bomb. His phone buzzed on the counter, making him jump. He snatched it up and stared at the screen.

"What the hell is that?" he whispered, eyes darting to the window. His brain was cycling through possibilities: a generator? A power surge? A fucking alien invasion?

He stood slowly, his chair scraping against the floor, and crept to the window. Carefully, he peeled back the blinds with two fingers.

The street outside was empty. Silent. Nothing unusual. No ominous black vans. No lurking shadowy figures. Nothing that explained the low, mechanical hum that was now setting his teeth on edge. "Alright, Paul, you're losing it," he muttered, letting the blinds fall back into place.

The hum stopped. The sudden silence was almost worse. It wrapped around him like a heavy blanket, thick and suffocating. He stared at the laptop, still sitting innocently on the table as if it weren't the source of all this insanity. His phone buzzed again. He nearly jumped out of his skin.

The text was from an unknown number: "Welcome to the game, Paul. You have one week to give the laptop away willingly. Failure to comply will have consequences."

He let out a breath he didn't realize he was holding. "One week?" he muttered. "Okay... okay, I can figure this out. That's not so bad." But then he thought about the video. The man's hollow stare. The way he said, "grave danger."

Paul slammed his phone down and paced the room. "One week to pass on a cursed laptop," he muttered, half-laughing, half-panicking. "Yeah, that's not ominous or fucking psychotic at all. What is this, a horror movie? 'Pass the haunted laptop before the ghost gets you?'"

His phone buzzed again, and he froze. The new text read, "Tick tock, Paul. Every second counts."

He glared at the phone. "Oh, fuck you. Seriously. What are you? Are you some discount Jigsaw wannabe?"

Paul grabbed the laptop and flipped it open. The text file that had been taunting him earlier was still on the screen. Unfamiliar words appeared as if being typed in real-time:

"Your cooperation is mandatory. Do not delay, Paul." He snapped the laptop shut. "Mandatory, my ass."

His phone buzzed again. He ignored it this time, too pissed off to play along. The room felt too quiet, the silence that made your skin crawl. He turned on the TV, flipping through channels to drown out his thoughts. Maybe he could pretend this wasn't happening. But the TV didn't cooperate. Every channel was static.

"What the hell?" he said, smacking the side of the remote.

The static cleared, and a distorted voice came through the speakers: "Paul, we don't appreciate defiance."

Paul jumped off the couch as if the sofa had just bitten him. "Jesus Christ!"

The screen flickered, and the exact words from his phone appeared on the TV: "One week, Paul. Do your job."

He ran to the TV and yanked the power cord. The TV went black. "That's it. I'm done. I'm not doing this bullshit," he said, pacing again. His mind raced with bad ideas: smash the laptop, toss it in the river, mail it to Antarctica. He considered all of them, knowing deep down none of them would work.

The laptop beeped. Against his better judgment, he opened it again. This time, the text on the screen sent a cold chill down his spine: "Congratulations, Paul. Your insubordination has earned you a new deadline: 24 hours to complete your task. You don't want to know what happens if you fail."

"WHAT?!" Paul shouted, kicking the leg of the table. "You can't just—no! You said one week!"

The laptop's screen flickered. "You did this to yourself, Paul. Don't blame us."

A low hum filled the room, vibrating through the walls. Paul froze. "No, no, no—don't start that shit again," he muttered, glancing toward the window.

He crept to the blinds and peeked outside. The street was dark, quiet, and empty—except for a faint glow in the sky. The hum grew louder.

Paul craned his neck, looking up. That's when he saw it. A sleek, black drone hovered just above the streetlight outside, its cloaking device flickering in and out. Beneath it, a mounted gun glinted in the glow of the light.

Paul's jaw dropped. "What the actual fuck?" The drone tilted slightly, its camera locking onto him like a predator sizing up its prey. A red laser dot appeared on his chest.

Paul stumbled backward, hands raised. "Okay! Okay! You win! Jesus Christ, I get it!"

The laser dot vanished. The drone hovered momentarily before silently ascending and disappearing into the night. Paul collapsed onto the couch, breathing hard. His phone buzzed again. He didn't even flinch this time.

The message read, "We're glad you understand the urgency. There are 23 hours and 55 minutes remaining."

He stared at the screen, his mind spinning. "These guys are fucking psycho." He thought to himself.

His phone buzzed again. “Tick tock, Paul. Time is precious.” The only thing he could think of doing was getting into his car and driving. Maybe he’d see someone, anyone, to give this laptop to. He grabbed his keys and the computer and left his apartment.

Chapter Four

Life on the Line

Paul's hands gripped the steering wheel as he drove aimlessly through the streets, the weight of the laptop sitting next to him like an anvil on his chest. His phone buzzed again. He didn't even look at it. He already knew what it would say: Tick tock, Paul. Time is precious. "Yeah, yeah, I fucking get it," he muttered.

"Time may be precious, but this shit has me hungry again," he said with a nervous chuckle. He pulled into the parking lot of a convenience store. He needed a drink—maybe five—to steady his nerves and help him think clearly. Walking into the store, Paul kept his head low. The fluorescent lights were too bright, and the background music was too cheerful for his current predicament.

His mind raced as he grabbed a couple of sandwiches and drinks from the fridge. How did I get here? Yesterday, my biggest problem was whether to get BBQ or sour cream chips. Now I'm running from murder drones and handing off cursed laptops like they're hot potatoes.

Paul reached the register and paid with shaky hands. The cashier barely looked at him as she handed him his change. "Have a nice day," she said, her voice robotic.

Paul almost laughed. "Yeah, sure, you too," he said, heading out the door. As he walked out, he noticed his car window had been shattered.

His heart sank. "No, no, no," he cried, running to the car and pushing the door open. Of course, the only thing missing from the vehicle was the laptop.

A wave of relief washed over him. For the first time in hours, he thought he was safe. *It's over*, he told himself. The cursed thing is out of my hands. He could almost breathe again. Then his phone buzzed. It was another message.

"You must retrieve the laptop, Paul. You must willingly give it to someone. Getting it taken isn't an option and will fail."

He spun around, scanning the parking lot. His stomach twisted into knots. "Shit!" he yelled, slamming his fist on the top of his car. A man was running down the block, cradling the laptop. "Hey!" Paul shouted, giving chase. "That's mine, you asshole!"

The man didn't stop. Paul cursed under his breath, adrenaline kicking in as he pushed himself to run faster. He wasn't athletic by any stretch, but the thought of losing the laptop—and whatever fresh hell the mystery people would throw at him for it—kept him moving.

The man darted into an alley, and Paul followed, gasping for air. "Drop the fucking laptop!" Paul yelled.

The man glanced back, sneering. "Go to hell!" Paul was about to yell something equally unhelpful when the hum started.

It was faint initially but grew louder, reverberating off the alley walls. Paul slowed, dread washing over him like ice water. The thief stopped, too, looking around in confusion. "What the—?"

The hum became a mechanical roar as a sleek black drone descended into view. The cloaking device flickered briefly before fully deactivating, revealing its mounted gun. "Holy shit!" the thief yelled.

Paul ducked behind a dumpster, peeking out just in time to see the red dot appear on the thief's chest. "Wait! No, no, no!" the thief screamed, holding his hands up.

The drone didn't wait. A single shot rang out, sharp and metallic, echoing in the narrow alley. The thief crumpled to the ground, blood pooling beneath him.

Paul stared wide-eyed, his heart pounding like a jackhammer. The drone hovered momentarily, its camera tilting toward Paul's hiding spot as if to say, You're welcome. Then it zipped away, vanishing into the night.

Paul stayed frozen for an eternity before finally crawling out from behind the dumpster.

The thief lay motionless, his hand still clutching the laptop. Paul stepped over the pool of blood, his shoes sticking slightly to the asphalt.

"Jesus Christ," he whispered, his stomach churning. He crouched down, pried the laptop from the thief's limp fingers, and immediately wiped his hands on his hoodie.

Sirens wailed in the distance. Paul's eyes darted toward the alley's opening. "Nope, nope, nope," he muttered, clutching the laptop to his chest and sprinting back toward his building.

When he got back to his apartment, he slammed the door shut and locked it. His legs gave out, and he sank to the floor, the laptop still in his hands.

His phone buzzed. He didn't want to look, but he couldn't help himself. "You see, Paul? We handle rule-breakers. Please don't disappoint us again. 21 hours, 15 minutes remaining."

Paul stared at the message, his hands shaking. He looked at the laptop, its black screen reflecting his pale, terrified face. "I hate you," he whispered to it. "I fucking hate you."

He dragged himself to the couch and collapsed, his body heavy with exhaustion and guilt. All he could see when he closed his eyes was the thief's face—the panic, the blood, the way he crumpled to the ground.

His phone buzzed again. "Tick tock, Paul. Make your choice." Paul lay there, staring at the ceiling, too exhausted to respond. He was running out of time and options and maybe—just maybe—out of soul.

Chapter Five

A Fatal Chain

Paul continued to lie on the floor of his apartment, staring at the ceiling as if it might suddenly offer him answers. The apartment was silent now, and the drone's hum and the chaos from earlier were nothing more than memories. But the silence wasn't comforting; it was suffocating.

He finally forced himself to sit up, his body heavy with exhaustion and guilt. The laptop sat on the table, still and quiet, like it hadn't been the center of a complete fucking nightmare just hours ago.

Paul rubbed his face with his hands, muttering, "Get up, Paul. Just get up."

It took effort, like dragging himself through wet concrete, but he stood. His legs felt weak, as if they might give out at any moment. He stumbled toward the door, grabbed his car keys, and looked back at the laptop one last time.

"You're the worst fucking thing that's ever happened to me," he whispered to it before heading out.

The cool night air hit him as he stepped out of his building. He climbed into his car, the seat creaking under his weight, and sat there momentarily. The steering wheel felt cold in his hands. He stared at the dashboard, his brain buzzing with endless, unanswerable questions.

Where was he supposed to go? What was he supposed to do? He didn't have a plan. He didn't even have a destination.

With a deep breath, Paul started the car and pulled out of the lot. He drove without thinking, the city streets blurring past him in streaks of orange streetlights and shadows. The laptop sat in the passenger seat, its case closed and harmless-looking, but Paul couldn't stop glancing at it. It felt alive, like it might leap at him if he wasn't careful.

"What the hell am I supposed to do with you?" he muttered, gripping the wheel tightly. His brain scrambled to come up with names, people he could hand this nightmare to.

He started talking aloud, his voice bitter and sarcastic. "What about Jerry? He'd probably think this whole thing was ARG or whatever nerd shit he's into. I mean, the guy spent $1,200 on miniature space marines last year—he'd probably pay me to take the laptop if I said it was haunted."

Paul shook his head. "No, he doesn't deserve it. And he'd probably fuck it up and get himself killed anyway." Next, his mind turned to his boss, Doug. That idea made him laugh, but not in a happy way. "Oh, yeah. Doug. Perfect. I'll stroll into work, hand him the laptop, and say, 'Hey, boss, I thought you might want this! Don't worry; it only comes with a minor chance of death by a drone strike!'"

He let out a hollow laugh. "Fucking Doug. He'd probably blame me for it anyway. Dock my pay for handing him a 'defective product.'" Paul's laugh faded into a sigh. There was no one. He had no friends close enough, no family nearby, and no coworkers dumb enough to fall for it. The sinking realization hit him hard: he was utterly alone in this.

He kept driving, aimless. The city felt deserted, like it had emptied just for him. Each passing block felt like another step toward nowhere.

Then he saw her. Up ahead, Stacy was pushing her cart along the sidewalk. Her mismatched clothes swayed as she walked, her familiar hum drifting faintly through the night air.

Paul slowed the car, his heart pounding. "No," he muttered, shaking his head. "No fucking way. Not her."

But the thought had already taken root in his mind. Stacy didn't have a phone. She didn't have a home. She didn't even have a mailbox.

She was practically a ghost in the system. In the twisted logic of this nightmare, she was... perfect.

Paul drove past her, his grip tightening on the wheel. "I can't do that to her," he muttered. "I can't." But then the memories came rushing back. The drone. The hum. The red dot on his chest.

The thief is lying in a pool of blood. Paul pulled over a block away and slammed the car into the park. His hands trembled as he leaned forward, resting his forehead on the steering wheel.

"Fuck," he whispered, the word coming out like a sob. He sat there, battling himself. Stacy didn't deserve this. She was kind, warm, and the closest thing to a friend he had outside of work.

But he couldn't ignore the ticking clock in his head. He couldn't ignore the growing sense of dread that the people behind this laptop wouldn't let him walk away if he failed.

He lifted his head and stared out the windshield. "I'm going to hell for this," he muttered, his voice shaking. Paul started the car and drove back toward her. As he pulled up beside her, Stacy turned and smiled when she saw him.

"Paul!" she said, beaming. "Twice in one day! You spoil me, honey."

Paul forced a laugh as he stepped out of the car, holding the laptop like it weighed a thousand pounds. "Hey, Stacy. Just... thought I'd stop by and see how you're doing."

"I'm doing just fine," she said, patting her cart. "Trying to keep busy, you know."

Paul nodded, swallowing hard. "Actually, uh, I've got something for you."

Stacy raised an eyebrow, curious. "For me? Paul, you don't have to—"

"It's a laptop," Paul said quickly, shoving it into her hands before he could think twice. "Someone left it at the shop past the claim date. I figured, you know, maybe you could use it."

Stacy looked at it like it was a treasure chest. "A laptop? For me? Oh, Paul, I couldn't—"

"Of course, you can," Paul said, smiling. "It's already set up. There's even a folder open with some fun stuff. Just check it out when you get a chance."

Stacy hugged the laptop to her chest, her eyes misting. "Paul, you're an angel. A real angel."

Paul's stomach churned, but he kept the smile plastered on his face. "Just enjoy it, okay? Stay safe out here."

"I will," Stacy said, grinning ear to ear. "Thank you, Paul. Really. You're a saint."

Paul nodded, backing toward his car. "Take care, Stacy," he said, his voice barely above a whisper. As he drove away, his phone buzzed.

"Congratulations, Paul. You've successfully handed it off; now we wait for her to open the file." Paul didn't feel well done. He felt like a piece of shit.

"Fucking fantastic," he muttered as he gripped the wheel, tears burning at the corners of his eyes.

Chapter Six

Paranoia

Paul barely remembered parking his car. When he stepped back into his apartment, the walls seemed to close around him. The air felt heavier, thicker like it was trying to suffocate him. He locked the door—deadbolt, chain, and all—and pressed his back against it, his chest heaving.

He stared at the laptop-shaped void on his table, where the cursed machine had sat for hours, taunting him, threatening to destroy his life. Now, it was gone. But the relief he expected to feel wasn't there. Instead, there was guilt. Stacy's smile flashed in his mind, her voice echoing: "You're an angel, Paul. A real saint."

"A saint," Paul muttered bitterly, kicking off his shoes and stumbling to the couch. "Yeah, sure. A saint who just handed her a fucking death sentence. Halo-worthy shit right there."

He collapsed onto the couch, staring at the ceiling. His phone buzzed in his pocket, but he didn't check it. He already knew it wasn't going to be good news. After a long moment, he finally sat up and pulled the phone out. The notification glared at him like an accusation:

"Congratulations, Paul. You've successfully passed the laptop. Stacy has one week."

"Fuck," he whispered, tossing the phone onto the coffee table. She opened the files. His hands dragged down his face, and for a second, he thought about punching something—anything—to feel something other than this gnawing pit in his stomach. Sunday. She had until Sunday.

Paul rubbed his temples, his thoughts spiraling. "You're not going to fix this," he muttered. "They'll kill you if you try." Still, the guilt wouldn't let him go. Maybe he could warn her. Perhaps he could figure out some way to help her.

Then his phone buzzed again, pulling him out of his thoughts. "We wouldn't recommend interference, Paul. You've seen what happens to rule-breakers."

Paul stared at the message, his mouth dry. His mind flashed back to the thief—the red dot, the shot, the blood pooling on the ground. They were watching him. Even now.

"Fuck you," he muttered at the phone, his voice trembling.

The following message came instantly: "Mind your language, Paul. You're safe... for now."

The "for now" sat there on the screen like a threat. He tossed the phone, watching it bounce off the armrest of a chair and hit the floor.

"This is fucking insane," he said, pacing the living room. His thoughts tumbled over each other too fast to make sense of. He felt like he was spiraling, like his brain was short-circuiting.

Every creak of the apartment made him jump. Every car passing by his window sent a shiver down his spine. The drone's hum haunted him, even in the silence. He started unplugging things. First, it is his TV, then his router, and then anything remotely electronic. He ripped the power strip from the wall, the cords tangling in his hands as he tossed them into a pile on the floor.

"No fucking way you're spying on me through this shit," he muttered. "Not today, you assholes." But the paranoia didn't stop there. He grabbed a roll of duct tape and went to work covering every camera in the apartment. His laptop, phone, and the ancient webcam he hadn't touched in years got taped over.

After what felt like an eternity, he stood in the middle of his living room, surrounded by unplugged electronics and scraps of duct tape. His heart was pounding, his mouth dry, and his hands wouldn't stop shaking.

"Calm down, Paul," he told himself, pacing again. "You're fine. They're done with you. They said you're safe." But the words didn't comfort him. He didn't trust them.

The hours dragged by. He tried lying on the couch, but every time he closed his eyes, he saw Stacy's face—or worse, her body lying in the park, bloodied and broken. He tried turning on the TV, but he'd unplugged it and wasn't about to risk plugging it back in.

So, he sat there silently, staring at the wall, his thoughts spiraling further into darkness. By Saturday morning, Paul looked like shit. His eyes were bloodshot, his hair was a mess, and his clothes smelled faintly of sweat and panic. He had missed work this whole time. He'd barely eaten, surviving on chips and soda because he didn't trust his microwave.

Every second felt like an eternity. He kept checking his phone for news, but there was nothing. No texts from the mysterious assholes behind the laptop. No breaking headlines about drone attacks. Just silence.

It wasn't until Sunday night that he finally turned his phone back on. He couldn't stop himself. He had to know. The screen lit up; he had missed calls from work but didn't care about work. Then his stomach twisted when he saw the notification from the news app:

"Breaking: Woman Found Dead in Homeless Encampment. Authorities Report Gunshot Wound to the Head." Paul's blood ran cold. He opened the article with trembling hands.

The report was vague, but he didn't need details to know. He could see it clearly in his mind: Stacy, lying on the ground, her cart overturned, the laptop nowhere in sight. Paul dropped the phone onto the couch and sat back, staring at the ceiling.

"I did that," he whispered, his voice cracking. "I fucking did that." The weight of it hit him all at once.

He buried his face in his hands, shaking, tears streaming down his cheeks. He'd survived, sure, but at what cost? They'd won. They probably always win. Paul felt utterly hollow for the first time since this nightmare started.

Chapter Seven

Survival Guilt

Paul didn't sleep that night—or the next. By Monday morning, he was even more a wreck. He hadn't showered; he barely ate anything. His apartment was still in shambles, every electronic device unplugged, and every camera taped over like he was preparing for a government raid.

His phone sat on the coffee table, mocking him. He stared at it like it might explode if he touched it. "You're fine," he muttered for the hundredth time. "They're done with you. They said you're safe. You did what they wanted."

The words rang hollow, like a bad punchline to a cruel joke. His brain kept going back to Stacy. The way her face lit up when he handed her the laptop. She'd hugged it to her chest like it was a lifeline. And now she was dead.

Paul buried his face in his hands, groaning. "You are a fucking coward," he whispered to himself. "You let them kill her. You let them fucking kill her." But what choice did he have? If he hadn't given her the laptop, they would've killed him instead. That was the part that haunted him most—the fact that, in the end, he chose himself.

He laughed bitterly, the sound dry and humorless. "Saint Paul, huh?" he muttered. "Patron fucking saint of passing the buck."

The laugh died in his throat as he glanced at the phone again. He hadn't heard from them since Friday, and there was no single message. Shouldn't that be a good thing? It didn't feel like it. By Tuesday, Paul finally forced himself to leave the apartment. He couldn't stay locked inside forever, no matter how much he wanted to. His paranoia had reached the point where even the walls felt like they were watching him.

He threw on a hoodie and sunglasses, more out of habit than actual need, and stepped outside for the first time in days. The sunlight was blinding, and the noise of the city was overwhelming. It felt like he was stepping into an alien world. As he walked down the street, his heart raced whenever a car drove past, or a shadow moved in the corner of his vision. He kept glancing at the sky, half-expecting to see another drone hovering above him, its gun pointed at his chest.

"You're being ridiculous," he muttered under his breath. "They're not going to waste their time on you. You're small potatoes. You did what they wanted, and now they've moved on to the next poor asshole."

That thought should've been comforting, but it wasn't. He stopped at a coffee shop, needing anything to ground him. The smell of burnt espresso and stale pastries filled the air as he stepped inside, the quiet hum of conversation contrasting with the chaos in his mind.

Paul ordered a black coffee, his voice shaking as he handed over his card. He waited by the counter, his hands twitching. Every time the door chimed, his heart jumped into his throat. When his coffee finally came, he grabbed it and bolted, ignoring the barista's polite "Have a nice day!"

"Yeah, you too," he muttered under his breath. "Hope you don't get handed a fucking murder laptop." He sat in his car, sipping the coffee and staring at nothing. For a moment, he felt almost normal. The sunlight streaming through the windshield, the bitter taste of the coffee, and the distant sound of traffic were almost enough to make him believe the last week had been a bad dream.

Then his phone buzzed. Paul froze. He stared at the phone like a coiled snake, his hand hovering over it. It had been days since their last message. Days of silence. Why now?

Slowly, he picked up the phone and unlocked the screen. It wasn't a message. It was a news alert.

"BREAKING: Identity of body found at Homeless Encampment: Woman's name is Claire Whitman." Paul's stomach twisted. He opened the article, his hands trembling.

"What the fuck?" he said. "Stacy's alive? She must have handed the laptop off hours after I gave it to her."

The news said, "No witnesses, no suspects." However, they did mention an abandoned laptop found at the scene.

Paul's blood ran cold. "Shit," he whispered, staring at the screen. His mind raced. Was the laptop still out there? His phone buzzed again. This time, it was a text.

"You're safe, Paul. Don't worry about the others." Paul's hand tightened around the phone, his knuckles turning white.

"Don't worry?" he said aloud, his voice rising. "Don't fucking worry? You think I'm just going to sit here and act like everything's fine while you keep killing people?"

Another message came through almost at once: "You did your part. Move on."

Paul threw the phone onto the passenger seat, his chest heaving. He wanted to scream, punch something, and do anything to make this stop. But he couldn't. He was trapped.

By the time he got back to his apartment, Paul was shaking. He locked the door behind him and collapsed onto the couch, his head in his hands. The messages stopped after that. There were no more texts, no more news alerts, just silence.

It should've been a relief, but it wasn't. The silence was worse. It gave him too much time to think, too much time to replay everything in his head. The laptop. The messages. The drone.

Paul stared at the ceiling, his thoughts spinning out of control. He knew he'd never be free of this. He wasn't done with them even if they were done with him. He laughed again, a bitter, humorless sound. "Fucking saint, huh?" he muttered. "Yeah. Saintly, Paul."

He reached for the bottle of whiskey he kept under the couch, unscrewed the cap, and took a long swig. The burn in his throat was a welcome distraction from the guilt eating him alive.

No amount of whiskey was going to make him forget, though. Nothing was. And deep down, Paul knew one thing for sure:

They weren't done with him.

Not yet.

Sarah

Hello Sarah

Chapter One

A Secret Admirer

Sarah leaned against the cool brick wall of the campus cafeteria, clutching her tray of half-eaten food. She had just finished her first week of classes, and the buzz of college life was exhilarating. Everywhere she looked, there were people—laughing, talking, running to catch a class. It was chaos, but it was her chaos now, and she loved it.

Her last class of the day, Introduction to Literature, quickly became her favorite. Dr. Caldwell was a charismatic professor who made poetry feel alive, dissecting every line like a puzzle waiting to be solved. She often stayed after class, jotting down notes and lingering over his feedback on her assignments.

Sarah's backpack felt heavier than usual as she returned to her dorm that afternoon. She shrugged it off, assuming she'd crammed too many books. When she finally got to her room, she unzipped the main pocket and stopped cold.

A piece of folded paper, meticulously creased, sat on her notebook. Curious, she unfolded it.

"Hello, Sarah. You looked lovely in class today. Your smile is radiant—don't ever hide it." Sarah blinked, reading the words over again. A slow smile spread across her face. A secret admirer?

"Who even does this anymore?" she muttered, cheeks flushed with embarrassment and excitement. She wasn't used to this kind of attention—high school had been uneventful, a blur of studying and trying not to be noticed too much.

Tucking the note back into her bag, she felt a small thrill run through her. She imagined some shy, romantic classmate slipping the letter into her bag when she wasn't looking. Maybe it was someone from her literature class—one of the guys who always sat in the back row, or perhaps even someone she hadn't noticed yet.

That evening, Sarah sat cross-legged on her bed, staring at the note. She couldn't stop thinking about who might have sent it. Kim, her roommate, was out, so she called Emma and Jake, her two best friends from high school, on a video chat.

"Okay, so, tell me who it is," Jake said as soon as Sarah held up the letter. He leaned closer to his camera, his sandy hair flopping over his forehead.

"I have no idea!" Sarah said, laughing. "But come on, this is kind of... sweet, right?"

"It's adorable," Emma said, brushing her dark curls out of her face. "It's so old-school romantic. You have a secret admirer, Sarah! Do you know how rare that is these days? You must find out who it is."

Jake smirked. "Or maybe it's someone unexpected. Like that guy who spilled coffee on you the other day. What's his name? Tim?" Sarah rolled her eyes.

"It wasn't Tim. He barely looked at me when he apologized."

"Well, whoever it is," Emma said, her tone teasing, "you must keep us updated. What if he writes you poetry next? This could be your college love story!"

"Maybe," Sarah said, grinning.

The following day, she was still thinking about the note. It was the first thing that popped into her head when she woke. She scanned the classroom during literature class, wondering if anyone was acting unusual or looking at her more than they should.

She thought about glancing back at the students seated behind her, but Dr. Caldwell's booming voice brought her focus back to the front of the room.

"Poetry," he said, "isn't just about words on a page. It's about connection—how you feel when someone else's words resonate with your soul."

Sarah scribbled the quote into her notebook, but her thoughts drifted back to the letter. Whoever had written it, they had noticed her smile. That meant they'd seen something in her worth noticing.

By the time the class ended, Sarah had convinced herself that her admirer must be thoughtful and observant. Maybe she'd get another letter soon. She didn't have to wait long.

That evening, Sarah found a second note tucked into her literature textbook. She almost didn't notice it, wedged between two pages she'd flipped open while studying.

"Hello, Sarah. You're even prettier when you're focused. I could watch you all day." Her breath caught as she read it. Unlike the first note, this one felt more personal—almost intimate.

She grabbed her phone and quickly texted Emma. "Another one. This is so weird but exciting."

Emma texted back almost at once. "No way! What does it say? Who is this mystery guy??"

Sarah smiled to herself, tucking the note back into the pages of her book. She didn't know who it was, but she had to admit: the idea of being admired, even anonymously, was thrilling. Little did she know, it was only the beginning.

Chapter Two

The Smile Fades

The next few days blurred together in a haze of classes, late-night study sessions, and coffee-fueled mornings. Sarah tried to focus on her work, but her mind was constantly preoccupied with the mysterious notes. She was intrigued and unnerved by the situation, and whenever she opened her bag or pulled a book off her shelf, she half-expected to find another one.

When she found the third letter, she was no longer surprised. It was waiting for her in her mailbox. Unlike the first two, which had been folded, this one was sealed in an envelope. The handwriting on the front was the same—neat, elegant, and deliberate. Her name was written in bold cursive.

She stood there for a moment, staring at the envelope. A strange feeling stirred in her chest—part excitement, part unease, growing more pronounced with each passing second. Slowly, she tore it open and pulled out the note inside.

"Hello, Sarah. That argument with your roommate wasn't worth it. You were right, though—she shouldn't leave dishes in the sink."

"What the fuck?" Sarah whispered. Her breath hitched, and the letter slipped from her hands, fluttering to the ground. Her heart pounded as she replayed last night's argument with Kim. It had been a stupid fight—Kim had left her dirty dishes piled up in the tiny dorm sink for the third day in a row, and Sarah, frustrated after a long day, had snapped. They'd exchanged a few sharp words before Kim stormed out, slamming the door behind her.

No one else had been there. No one could have overheard. Sarah picked up the letter with trembling fingers. This wasn't a coincidence. Someone knew. Someone had been there.

That evening, Sarah sat on her bed, the three letters in front of her like puzzle pieces. The first two had seemed sweet, even flattering. But this one was different. This one felt invasive, almost predatory. The change in tone was unmistakable, sending a shiver down her spine.

Her phone buzzed with a call from Emma. She answered immediately, needing to hear a friendly voice. "Another one?" Emma asked without preamble.

"Yes," Sarah said, her voice shaking. "But Emma... it's fucking creepy this time. It's not like the others."

"What does it say?" Emma asked.

Sarah hesitated, then read the letter aloud. There was silence on the other end of the line.

Finally, Emma spoke. "That's not okay, Sarah. How would they even know about that fight?"

"I don't know," Sarah whispered.

"Have you told Jake?" asked Emma.

Sarah hesitated, "No, not yet."

Emma frowned, "Well, you need to. And honestly, you should tell someone on campus. This is getting fucking weird."

The following day, Sarah told Jake everything. They sat in the campus café, the letters between them on the sticky table. Jake frowned as he read them, his typically playful demeanor replaced with a serious expression.

"This isn't funny anymore," he said, looking up at her. "You're sure no one could've overheard you and your roommate?"

Sarah shook her head, "The door was shut. Kim and I were the only ones there."

Jake ran a hand through his hair, staring at the letters. "Okay, so this person either knows you well or... they've been watching you."

Sarah's stomach turned. "Watching me?" she repeated, her voice barely audible.

Jake shrugged helplessly. "I mean, how the fuck else would they know all this stuff?"

Sarah rubbed her arms, trying to fight off the creeping sense of dread. She felt exposed as if she were being seen even now.

"I think Emma's right," Jake said finally. "You need to go to campus security."

That night, Sarah lay in bed, staring at the ceiling. She hadn't gone to campus security yet. Something about it felt too drastic, like admitting aloud that this was more than a harmless prank. She told herself she'd wait a little longer to see if the letters stopped. But sleep didn't come quickly. Every noise in the hallway made her jump. Every creak of the floorboards made her hold her breath.

At one point, she thought she heard footsteps outside her door. She sat up, clutching her blankets, straining to listen. There was nothing—just silence.

Still, she couldn't shake the feeling that someone was there, just on the other side of the door, watching and waiting.

The fourth letter came the next day. This time, it was taped to her dorm room door.

"Hello, Sarah. You shouldn't be out so late. Someone could hurt you. You don't want that, do you?"

Her hands shook as she ripped the letter down, her heart pounding. This wasn't romantic. This wasn't sweet. This was a fucking threat. She could feel her fear turning into anger, a fierce determination not to let this anonymous admirer intimidate her.

She stormed into her room, locking the door behind her. She immediately called Emma and Jake, her voice trembling with fear and anger. She held the phone so tightly that her knuckles turned white.

"Another one," she said as soon as they answered. "It's on my door. They're watching me."

"What does it say?" Jake asked, his voice sharp.

Sarah read the note aloud. There was a long pause.

Then Emma said, "You need to report this. Right now. No more fucking waiting."

Jake agreed. "This is getting dangerous, Sarah. Whoever this is, they're not just some harmless admirer. This is some serious shit."

Sarah nodded, though they couldn't see her. "Okay," she said, her voice barely a whisper. "Okay, I'll go."

But as she hung up the phone and stared at the letter in her hand, she couldn't shake the feeling that whoever was behind this wasn't just watching. They were getting closer.

Chapter Three

A Note Too Far

Sarah's nerves frayed when she walked into the small campus security office. She clutched her backpack tightly, the letters stuffed inside like evidence in a crime show.

The officer at the desk looked up from his computer, a tired expression on his face. "Can I help you?"

"Yeah," Sarah said, her voice wavering. "I... I've been getting these letters. They're anonymous, and they're—" She hesitated. "They're threatening me now."

The officer raised an eyebrow, clearly unimpressed. "Threatening you? How so?"

Sarah pulled out the most recent letter and slid it across the desk. The officer picked it up, reading it slowly. When he was done, he set it down and looked at her. "This could just be someone messing with you," he said flatly. "You know, a prank. College students pull this kind of stuff all the time."

"A prank?" Sarah repeated, her voice rising. "Does this look like a fucking prank to you?"

The officer held up his hands defensively. "I'm not saying it's not serious, but unless you know who's doing it or have proof that someone's following you, there's not much we can do."

Sarah's stomach twisted with frustration. "So, you're saying I just have to wait until something worse happens before you'll do anything?"

He sighed. "Look, I'll note this and let the patrol officers know to keep an eye on your building. But I'm telling you, it's probably just some jerk trying to scare you."

Sarah snatched the letter back, stuffing it into her bag. "Thanks for nothing," she muttered as she walked out. When she returned to her dorm, Sarah called Jake immediately, her anger bubbling under the surface.

"They didn't do shit," she said as soon as he picked up.

"What do you mean?" Jake asked. "I mean, they don't care!" she snapped. "They said it's probably a prank and told me to deal with it."

"That's fucking bullshit," Jake said. "What if this person does something? They're just going to wait until it's too late?"

"That's exactly what I said." Sarah sighed, rubbing her temples.

"I don't know what to do, Jake. This isn't stopping. It's getting worse." Jake hesitated before speaking.

"Okay, listen. We'll figure this out. Emma and I will help you. You're not dealing with this alone, okay?"

"Okay," Sarah said quietly. That night, Sarah kept her curtains shut and her door double locked. She tried to study, but every sound in the hallway made her jump. Her paranoia felt suffocating, wrapping around her like a vice.

When she finally climbed into bed, she couldn't stop replaying the officer's dismissive tone. It's probably just a prank. The words echoed like a taunt. At some point, she drifted off, but her sleep was restless and filled with strange, fragmented dreams. She dreamed of shadows moving outside her window, her door creaking open while she was frozen in bed, unable to scream.

She woke up gasping, her heart pounding in her chest. The room was dark, but something felt wrong. She sat up slowly, her breath hitching as her eyes scanned the room. Everything looked normal—the desk piled with books, the faint glow of her phone on the nightstand—but the fear and vulnerability wouldn't go away.

And then she heard footsteps—slow and deliberate, just outside her door. Sarah froze, her blood turning to ice. She sat perfectly still, straining to listen to her heart pounding. The suspense was palpable as the footsteps paused directly before her door.

For a moment, everything was silent. Then, a soft scraping sound—like something being slipped under the door. Sarah's breath caught in her throat. She didn't move until the footsteps faded down the hallway. Finally, she forced herself to get up, her legs trembling. She reached for the small strip of paper from under the door and pulled it into the room.

It was another note: "Hello, Sarah. You locked your door. Smart girl, but locks can be broken."

"Fuck," Sarah whispered, dropping the note as if it had burned her. Her chest heaved as panic set in, her desperation for help growing. Whoever this was, they weren't just watching her anymore—they were testing her, pushing her boundaries. She grabbed her phone and dialed Emma. When she answered, Sarah didn't even wait for a hello.

"He was here," she said, her voice shaking. "Outside my fucking door."

Emma's sharp intake of breath crackled through the phone. "What? Are you okay? What did he do?"

"He slipped another note under the door. He said..." Sarah swallowed hard, trying to steady herself. "He said locks can be broken."

"Jesus fucking Christ," Emma said. "This is insane. You're not staying there alone, Sarah. You're coming to my place tonight, okay? Pack a bag and get the hell out of there."

Sarah didn't argue. She grabbed her backpack, shoved some clothes into it, and bolted out the door, her heart pounding every step. She didn't know who was doing this or what they wanted, but one thing was clear: they wouldn't stop.

Chapter Four

A Kindness that Cuts

Sarah sat through her "Introduction to Literature" class the following day, barely hearing a word of Dr. Caldwell's lecture. Her mind was trapped in a loop of fear and exhaustion, the threat from the latest note echoing in her head: Locks can be broken.

She'd barely slept the night before, staying at Emma's apartment instead of her dorm. But even there, she couldn't shake the feeling that someone was watching her, lurking just outside her line of sight. Her hands shook as she took notes, her pen scratching uneven lines across the page.

Dr. Caldwell's voice boomed across the room, his usual passionate cadence dissecting a Shakespearean sonnet. Usually, Sarah loved how he taught; his enthusiasm was infectious, and his insights were sharp. But today, it was all noise.

"Sarah," Dr. Caldwell said suddenly, his voice snapping her back to reality. Her head jerked up.

"Y-yes?" He smiled, though there was a flicker of concern in his eyes. "What do you think Shakespeare is trying to say about vulnerability here?"

Sarah blinked, realizing she had no idea what he was talking about. The entire room felt like it was watching her, waiting for an answer. Her throat tightened.

"I, um... I think he's saying it's... dangerous to trust people?" she stammered, her words rushed and clumsy.

Dr. Caldwell tilted his head thoughtfully, then nodded. "Interesting perspective. Vulnerability can be dangerous, but it can also lead to profound connections. It's a balancing act, isn't it?"

He moved on, but Sarah could still feel the heat of her classmates' stares. She hunched over her notebook, willing the class to end. When the lecture ended, Sarah gathered her things as quickly as possible, hoping to slip out unnoticed. But before she could leave, Dr. Caldwell called her name.

"Sarah, could you stay for a moment?" Her stomach sank.

"Sure," she said, forcing a smile she didn't feel. The last students filed out, leaving the room empty except for her and Dr. Caldwell. He leaned against his desk, folding his arms as he studied her.

"You've been distracted lately," he said, his tone gentle but probing. "Is everything all right?"

Sarah hesitated, gripping her bag. For a moment, she thought about confiding in Dr. Caldwell, who always seemed to care for his students genuinely and might be able to help.

But then she thought about the campus security officer's dismissive reaction and the words caught in her throat. What if Dr. Caldwell thought she was overreacting, too? What if he didn't take her seriously?

"I'm fine," she said quickly. "Just... a little stressed."

Dr. Caldwell nodded, though his expression was unconvincing. "College can be overwhelming, especially in the first semester. But if something's bothering you, my office is always open. Sometimes it helps to talk it out."

Sarah forced another smile. "Thanks, Dr. Caldwell. I appreciate it." He held her gaze for a moment longer, his eyes searching hers, then nodded.

"Take care of yourself, Sarah." As Sarah returned to Emma's apartment, her mind churned with doubt. Maybe she should have said something to Dr. Caldwell. Perhaps he would have taken her seriously.

But then again, what could he even do? She didn't know who sent the letters or how to stop them. The whole situation felt like it was spinning out of her control.

When she reached Emma's place, Jake was already there, sprawled on the couch with a can of soda in hand. He looked up as Sarah walked in, his expression darkening when he saw the look on her face. "You, okay?" he asked.

Sarah dropped her bag on the floor and collapsed into a chair. "Dr. Caldwell asked if I was okay after class. I almost told him everything." Emma, who was perched on the arm of the couch, frowned. "Why didn't you?"

"I don't know," Sarah admitted. "I guess I didn't think he'd believe me. And even if he did, what could he do about it?"

Jake leaned forward, setting his soda on the coffee table. "I mean, he is a professor. If he believed you, he could put pressure on the administration or something. It's better than just sitting on your hands, Sarah."

Emma nodded. "Yeah. And he seems like a good guy. You might be surprised."

Sarah sighed, rubbing her temples. "Maybe. I just... I don't want to drag more people into this if it's nothing."

"It's not nothing," Jake said, his voice firm. "This person is stalking you, Sarah. They're leaving creepy-ass notes, they know where you live, and they're threatening you. That's not 'nothing.'"

"Jake's right," Emma said softly. "You can't keep this to yourself, Sarah. You need to let people help you." Sarah nodded reluctantly, though the knot of anxiety in her stomach didn't loosen.

Later that night, as she lay on the air mattress Emma had set up in her living room, Sarah stared at the ceiling, replaying Dr. Caldwell's words.

"My office is always open." He had seemed so earnest, so concerned. But a small, nagging voice in her mind whispered that maybe it was too late to trust anyone.

The thought made her stomach twist. She squeezed her eyes shut, trying to banish the doubt. But deep down, she couldn't shake the feeling that this nightmare was far from over.

Chapter Five

Subtle Shadows

Sarah sat on the edge of the air mattress in Emma's small apartment, staring at her phone. The cheap fabric squeaked as she shifted, trying to quiet the buzzing in her head. Despite Emma's best attempts to make her feel safe, she hadn't slept much. The apartment's thin walls did little to block out the sounds of the world outside, and every noise made her flinch.

Emma appeared in the doorway with two mugs of coffee. She handed one to Sarah, her expression soft but serious. "How'd you sleep?"

Sarah shook her head. "Barely."

Emma nodded knowingly, sitting beside her on the tiny futon that doubled as a couch. "You're not going to class, are you?"

"No," Sarah said, her voice firmer than she expected. "I can't. I just... I can't sit there pretending everything's normal. Not after..." Her words trailed off, but Emma understood.

Emma sipped her coffee, then placed the mug on the floor beside her. "You don't have to explain. Take the day. You need it."

A knock at the door interrupted them. Sarah flinched, her heart racing, but Emma stood up. "Relax. It's just Jake."

She opened the door, and Jake stepped inside, holding a paper bag that smelled like bagels and eggs. "Figured you could use some real food," he said, tossing the bag onto the counter. "You look like hell, Sarah."

"Gee, thanks," Sarah muttered, but her lips twitched into a weak smile.

Jake grabbed one of the bagels and perched on the armrest of the futon. "You're skipping class, huh?"

Sarah nodded, wrapping her hands around her coffee mug. "I just need a break."

"Good," Jake said. "You've been through enough. Let Caldwell deal with class on his own."

At the mention of Dr. Caldwell, Sarah stiffened, her grip on the mug tightening. Jake noticed and frowned. "What? Did something else happen?"

"No," Sarah said quickly. "I mean, not really. I just..." She hesitated. "I don't know. Something about him feels... off."

Emma raised an eyebrow. "Off how?"

"I don't know," Sarah repeated, frustration creeping into her voice. "I just don't trust him. He's been too attentive, too... interested."

Jake exchanged a glance with Emma but didn't press further. "Well, you're not alone here. We've got your back."

Later that afternoon, Sarah left Emma's apartment to grab a few things from her dorm. She moved quickly, keeping her head down and avoiding any familiar faces. She didn't want to explain why she wasn't in class or looked like she hadn't slept in days.

As she was leaving the building, she saw him—Dr. Caldwell. He was leaning casually against a wall near the entrance, scrolling on his phone. When he looked up and saw her, his face lit with what could only be described as concern.

"Sarah," he called out, slipping his phone into his pocket. "I didn't see you in class this morning."

Her heart skipped a beat. She forced a small smile, clutching her bag tightly. "Yeah, I just... wasn't feeling like myself today," she said. "Needed a break."

Dr. Caldwell nodded slowly, his gaze lingering on her. "I understand. Remember, if you need anything—or if there's something you want to discuss—my office is always open."

Sarah nodded again, her smile strained. "Thanks," she said quickly, turning to leave.

But something about his tone replayed in her mind as she walked away. *My office is always open.* The words still felt too deliberate, too calm, almost rehearsed. The pit in her stomach grew as she quickened her pace, not daring to look back.

That evening, Sarah sat on Emma's sofa while Jake leaned against the counter, munching on another bagel. She recounted her encounter with Dr. Caldwell, her voice trembling slightly as she repeated his words.

"'My office is always open,'" Jake repeated, frowning. "Yeah, that's... kind of weird."

"It's not just the words," Sarah said, shaking her head. "It's how he said it. Like... like he was inviting me for something more than just a chat."

Emma crossed her arms, her brow furrowed. "Do you think he's connected to the letters?"

"I don't know," Sarah admitted. "But I can't stop thinking about it. The way he looks at me, the way he's always... there. What if he knows something? What if he's involved?"

Jake set the bagel down and leaned forward. "If you're uncomfortable around him, trust your gut. But if he's involved, we need to figure out why. And what he wants."

Emma nodded. "Just don't be alone with him, Sarah. Promise us."

"I won't," Sarah said, her voice barely above a whisper. But even as she promised, she couldn't shake the memory of his calm and deliberate voice telling her that his office was always open.

And somewhere deep inside her, she knew she wasn't done with Dr. Caldwell. Not yet.

Chapter Six

Office Hours

Sarah sat outside Dr. Caldwell's office, her leg bouncing nervously. The beige walls of the faculty wing felt suffocating, and the faint hum of the fluorescent lights above made her feel like she was in some interrogation room.

What the hell was she doing here? This was a mistake. She shouldn't have come alone. But she had to know.

Her heart was pounding in her chest as she replayed the last few days in her head—the notes, the eerie familiarity of the handwriting, the way he kept asking if she was "okay." It all pointed to him. Didn't it? Or was she losing her fucking mind?

"Sarah," his voice called out. She flinched, her head snapping up. Dr. Caldwell stood in the doorway, smiling that same warm, practiced smile he always wore in class. "Come in," he said, holding the door open.

Her feet felt like lead as she walked into his office. The walls had bookshelves stacked high with old volumes, papers, and framed certificates. His desk was neat, with every piece of paper in its place and a steaming mug of coffee resting on the corner. "Have a seat," he said, gesturing to the chair before his desk.

She hesitated before sitting, her hands gripping her bag tightly in her lap. "So," he began, leaning back in his chair, his expression friendly but curious. "What's on your mind?"

For a moment, Sarah couldn't speak. Her throat felt dry, and her pulse thundered in her ears. She could feel his eyes on her, studying her, making her skin crawl. "I... I just wanted to talk," she said, her voice barely above a whisper.

He nodded, folding his hands on the desk. "Of course. Is everything okay? You've seemed... distracted in class lately." There it was again—that same question, that same concerned tone. Her chest tightened.

"Dr. Caldwell," she said, forcing herself to meet his gaze. "Have you... ever sent me a letter?" His expression didn't change, but there was the slightest flicker in his eyes, a barely perceptible shift that made her stomach drop.

"A letter?" he asked, tilting his head slightly. "What do you mean?"

"You know what I mean," she said, trembling. "The letters I've been getting. Someone's been leaving them for me—on my door, in my bag. They know things about me. Private things."

He leaned forward slightly, his brow furrowing. "Sarah, I'm not sure what you're talking about. Are you saying you think I—"

"I don't know what to think," she interrupted, her voice rising. "But the handwriting—it looks like yours. And you keep asking if I'm okay, like you know something's wrong. So, tell me the fucking truth. Is it you?"

For a long moment, he didn't speak. The silence was suffocating, and Sarah felt the air in the room grow heavier. Then, slowly, he smiled.

It wasn't the warm, reassuring smile she was used to. This one was different. It was cold, calculating. "Sarah," he said softly, his tone almost patronizing. "You've misunderstood something."

Her blood ran cold. "What does that mean?" she demanded, her voice shaking.

"It means," he said, standing up and walking around the desk, "you're making accusations that aren't true. I understand you're stressed, but you shouldn't let your imagination get the better of you."

She stood up, backing away as he approached. "I'm not imagining anything," she snapped. "I know it's you. I don't know how, but I fucking know."

He stopped a few feet away from her, his hands in his pockets, his smile never faltering. "Sarah," he said gently, "you're upset. You're scared. I understand that. But you need to be careful about what you're saying. False accusations can have grave consequences."

Her heart was pounding so hard she thought it might burst. Every instinct in her body screamed at her to run, to get out of there, but she couldn't move. "You think I don't know?" she said, her voice cracking. "You think I don't see the way you look at me? The way you fucking—"

"Stop," he said sharply, his voice cutting through the air like a knife. Sarah froze, her breath hitching. The friendly facade was gone now, replaced by something colder, darker.

"You don't know anything," he said, his voice low and steady. "You're just a scared little girl looking for someone to blame. And if you keep pushing this, you will regret it."

Her blood turned to ice. He took a step closer, and she stumbled back, her hands gripping the edge of the chair for support. "Stay away from me," she said, her voice trembling. "I swear to God if you come near me—"

"You'll what?" he asked, his smile returning, twisted and mocking. "Go to the administration? The police? Do you think they'll believe you?"

Tears burned in her eyes, but she refused to let them fall. She forced herself to stand tall, her voice steadier now. "I'll make them believe me. And I'll make sure everyone knows what you are."

He stared at her for a long moment, his expression unreadable. Then he stepped back, raising his hands in mock surrender.

"Do what you need to do, Sarah," he said, his voice calm again. "But remember this—you're not as smart as you think."

Without another word, she turned and bolted for the door, her heart pounding. Sarah didn't stop running until she was outside, the frigid air stinging her lungs. She doubled over, gasping for breath, her hands shaking uncontrollably. It was him. She knew it now. The way he'd looked at her, the way he'd tried to twist everything around—it was him.

But he was right about one thing: she needed proof. And she wasn't going to stop until she got it.

Chapter Seven

Proof in the Shadows

Sarah slammed the door to Emma's apartment, her breath still ragged from running. Jake and Emma both looked up from the couch, startled by the force of her entrance.

"Jesus, Sarah, what the fuck happened?" Jake asked, sitting up straight.

"It's him," Sarah said, her voice shaking as she paced the room. "It's Dr. Caldwell. It's fucking him. I knew it."

Emma stood up, her face pale. "What did he do? Did he admit it?"

"No, but he didn't deny it either. He... he kept trying to twist things around, acting like I'm making shit up. And then he fucking threatened me. He said I'd regret it if I kept pushing."

Jake's jaw tightened. "That son of a bitch. What the hell is wrong with him?"

Sarah stopped pacing, her fists clenched. "I'm not crazy. I know it's him. He's been watching me this whole time, leaving those notes, making me feel like I'm losing my mind. But he's right about one thing—I don't have proof. Not yet."

Emma's eyes widened. "What are you going to do?"

Sarah took a deep breath, trying to steady herself. "I'm going to his office. Tonight."

Jake stared at her. "What the fuck are you talking about?"

"I need proof," she said firmly. "If he's the one sending the letters, there's got to be something in his office—drafts, copies, something. And if I can find it, I can go to the administration or the police, and they'll have to take me seriously."

"That's fucking insane," Jake said, standing up. "What if he catches you? Or worse, what if he's already waiting for you?"

"Then I'll deal with it," Sarah snapped. "I'm not letting him get away with this. I'm done being scared."

Emma hesitated, glancing between Sarah and Jake.

"If you're going to do this... we're coming with you."

"No," Sarah said quickly. "I'm not dragging you all into this. It's my problem."

"Bullshit," Jake said. "We're not letting you go in there alone. What if something goes wrong? You need backup."

Emma nodded. "Jake's right. We'll stand watch or something, but you're not doing this alone."

Sarah hesitated but saw their determined expressions. She sighed. "Fine. If things go wrong, promise you'll leave."

Neither of them answered. "Promise me," she repeated, her voice hard.

"Yeah, fine," Jake muttered. "But we're not leaving unless you do."
The campus was eerily quiet that night, the darkened hallways of the faculty building lit only by the occasional flicker of a fluorescent light. Every step they took echoed, stretching Sarah's nerves to breaking.

Emma and Jake stayed by the entrance, watching Sarah walk down the hall toward Dr. Caldwell's office. Her palms were sweaty, and her heart pounded so loudly she was sure it would give her away.

When she reached his office door, she paused, her breath catching. The door was locked, as she'd expected. She pulled out the bobby pin she'd brought, her hands trembling as she tried to force it into the lock.

"Hurry the fuck up," she whispered to herself, glancing over her shoulder. Finally, the lock clicked, and she opened the door just enough to slip inside. The room smelled faintly of coffee and old books, as it always did. She closed the door quietly behind her, her eyes scanning the space.

The desk was the prominent place to start. She moved quickly, opening drawers and rifling through papers. Most of it was expected—class schedules, student assignments, a pile of essays he hadn't graded yet. "Come on, come on," she muttered, her frustration mounting.

And then she found it. A folder was in the bottom drawer beneath a stack of notebooks. She pulled it out and opened it, her stomach twisting as she saw what was inside.

Photographs. Of her.

Some were taken on campus—walking to class, sitting in the library, laughing with Emma and Jake. Others were more invasive. A shot of her sitting on her bed was taken through her dorm window. Another shows her walking alone at night, her head down, unaware of the camera.

Her hands shook as she flipped through the photos, bile rising in her throat. "Fucking psycho," she whispered, her voice trembling with rage.

Tucked in the back of the folder were handwritten pieces of paper. She pulled one out and immediately recognized the neat, looping cursive. It was one of the letters. She stared at it, a mix of fury and terror flooding her veins. This was it. This was the proof she needed.

But before she could grab the folder and leave, she heard footsteps. Her heart stopped. She froze, listening as the footsteps grew louder and closer. They stopped just outside the door. "Fuck," she whispered, panic setting in.

The doorknob rattled, and Sarah's mind raced. She shoved the folder back into the drawer, closing it as quietly as possible before ducking behind the desk. She pressed herself against the wood, her breathing shallow, and her hands gripped the edge of the desk so tightly that her knuckles turned white.

The door creaked open. She heard the slow, deliberate sound of someone walking into the room. The footsteps stopped, and she could feel the weight of their presence.

"Sarah," Dr. Caldwell's voice called softly, almost singing and drawing out her name.

Her blood turned to ice. "I know you're in here," he said, calm but dripping with malice. "You shouldn't have come. You don't know what you're doing."

She clamped a hand over her mouth, trying to stifle her breathing.

He moved closer, his footsteps slow and methodical. "You think you're so smart, don't you?" he said. "Coming in here, snooping through my things. But you don't understand, Sarah. This isn't a game."

She could see his shadow now, stretching across the floor as he moved around the desk. Her heart pounded so hard she thought it might give her away. She reached into her bag, her fingers closing around the can of pepper spray Emma had given her.

"I told you to stop," he continued, his voice dropping to a low growl. "But you didn't listen." He rounded the desk, and their eyes met. For a moment, time seemed to stop.

And then she moved. In one swift motion, she raised the pepper spray and sprayed it directly into his face. Dr. Caldwell let out a guttural scream, stumbling back and clutching his eyes.

"You fucking bitch!" he roared, his voice muffled by his hands. Sarah didn't wait. She bolted for the door, her heart racing as she threw it open and ran down the hall.

"Jake! Emma!" she screamed, her voice echoing. They were waiting by the entrance, their faces pale when they saw her running toward them. "Go! He's coming!" she shouted.

The three ran out of the building, the chilly night air hitting Sarah like a slap. She didn't stop until they were far away, her chest heaving, her hands still clutching the pepper spray.

"We need to call the fucking cops," Jake said, his voice shaky.

Sarah nodded, tears streaming down her face. “We have the proof now. He’s done.” But even as she said the words, she couldn’t shake the feeling that this wasn’t over. Not yet.

Chapter Eight

A Knock at the Door

Sarah sat on Emma's couch, knees pulled to her chest, and the air in the apartment was so heavy with tension that it felt suffocating. Jake paced back and forth, his phone clenched as he barked at the police dispatcher. Emma sat beside Sarah, her trembling hand resting on Sarah's arm, but even her touch couldn't offer comfort.

"We've told you everything!" Jake snarled into the phone. "He's stalking her. He's got photos of her in his office—photos he took through her window! What the hell else do you need to take this seriously?"

Sarah barely heard him. The memory of Dr. Caldwell's office was burned into her mind—the photographs, the letters, the moment he stepped through the door and saw her there. The venom in his voice echoed endlessly: *You think you're smart, don't you?* The weight of those words twisted in her chest.

"They said they'll send someone by tomorrow," Jake said, throwing his phone onto the coffee table with a loud *clatter*. "Tomorrow. Because stalking isn't urgent enough for these assholes."

Emma's grip tightened. "We shouldn't be alone tonight. We can all stay here," she said, her voice shaking.

Jake nodded sharply. "Yeah. We lock this place down. Windows, doors, everything. He's out there, and I don't think he's done."

The night was restless. Sarah lay in Emma's bed, staring at the pepper spray she'd placed on the nightstand. It was within arm's reach but didn't make her feel safer. Every creak of the apartment, every gust of wind outside, felt like a threat. She closed her eyes, but Dr. Caldwell's twisted smile awaited her. *You've humiliated him. You've made him angry. And he doesn't like being outsmarted.*

The following day, Sarah was jolted awake by a frantic knock at the door. She sat up, her heart pounding in her chest. Dozing on the couch, Jake shot up and hurried to the peephole. He froze.

"It's him," Jake whispered, his voice tight. "It's fucking him."

Sarah's blood ran cold. "What?"

"Dr. Caldwell," Jake said, glancing at her. "He's right outside."

Emma's face turned pale. "What the fuck does he want?"

Jake didn't answer. Instead, he grabbed a chair and jammed it under the doorknob. The knocking grew louder, more insistent. Then came his voice: calm, measured, and deeply unsettling.

"Sarah," Dr. Caldwell called. "We need to talk."

"Fuck off!" Jake shouted. "We're calling the cops!"

Dr. Caldwell chuckled, the sound low and almost amused. "Go ahead. Do you think they'll do anything? Sarah and I need to settle this ourselves."

Sarah stood frozen in the bedroom doorway. His voice had a weight to it, deliberate and savoring, as though he enjoyed the fear it caused. Her breath hitched as he called her name again, his tone almost affectionate.

"Sarah... You made a mistake coming into my office. But I'll forgive you if you open the door."

Jake grabbed a kitchen knife, his jaw tight. "I swear to God, if you try to come in here, I'll gut you."

Another chuckle. "Jake, Jake... So loyal, but you don't understand. She's in far deeper than you realize."

Emma's trembling hands fumbled with her phone as she dialed 911. "He's here," she said, her voice cracking. "He's outside our door right now."

For a moment, there was silence. Then, the knocking stopped.

The wait for the police felt like an eternity. Sarah kept glancing at the windows, sure his face would appear any moment. When the officers finally arrived, Jake let them in, his hand still gripping the knife.

"He was here," Emma said, her voice trembling. "Dr. Caldwell. He was calling for Sarah."

One of the officers nodded. "We'll search the area, but for now, you're safe."

"Safe?" Sarah snapped, her voice sharp. "He's not gone. He's not going to stop."

The officers exchanged uneasy looks before leaving to patrol the area. Emma locked every window and door while Jake took up position by the front door, knife still in hand.

That night, the apartment was plunged into an oppressive silence. Sarah lay awake, her ears straining for any sound. Exhaustion finally overtook her, but it wasn't long before she was pulled from sleep by the sound of heavy footsteps in the hallway. Her heart stopped.

"Emma?" she whispered, her voice trembling. No response.

She slid out of bed, her bare feet hitting the cold floor. The footsteps stopped just outside the bedroom door. Her breath hitched as the doorknob began to turn.

"Jake?" she called, her voice barely audible.

The door creaked open, and there he was. Dr. Caldwell stood in the dim light, his face calm but his eyes burning with something dark and unhinged.

"Hello, Sarah," he said softly.

She grabbed the pepper spray from the nightstand, but before she could react, he lunged forward. His hand clamped around her wrist, slamming it against the wall. The can clattered to the floor.

"You think you're clever," he hissed, his grip tightening. "But you don't understand. You're mine, Sarah. You've always been mine."

She struggled, twisting and kicking, but he was too strong. His face was inches from hers, his voice low and venomous. "You ruined everything. Did you think you could walk away from me?"

"Get the fuck off her!" Jake roared, charging into the room. He tackled Dr. Caldwell, sending them both crashing to the floor. Sarah stumbled back; her vision blurred with tears.

"Run, Sarah!" Jake shouted as he wrestled with Dr. Caldwell.

She bolted from the room, screaming for Emma. Behind her, the sound of struggle filled the apartment—grunts, shouts, the dull thud of fists. Then, silence.

Sarah turned back just in time to see Dr. Caldwell rise to his feet, a knife in his hand, blood dripping from the blade. Jake lay motionless on the floor.

"Jake!" Sarah screamed.

Dr. Caldwell's calm, eerie demeanor returned as he looked at her. "He was in the way. But now, it's just us."

Footsteps thundered from the hallway. The police burst through the door, guns drawn. "Drop the knife!" one of them shouted.

Dr. Caldwell smiled, his gaze locked on Sarah. "This isn't our goodbye, Sarah." He dropped the knife, raising his hands.

As officers cuffed him and led him away, Sarah ran to Jake, tears streaming down her face. "He's alive," Emma whispered, her hands pressing against his wound. "He's alive."

Chapter Nine

Tomorrow Starts Today

Later, the waiting room at the hospital was filled with palpable tension. In contrast to Sarah's motionless figure in a plastic chair, Emma's restless pacing and hurried handwriting painted a picture of their inner turmoil. Each second felt like an eternity. When the doctor finally emerged, they both leaped to their feet, their anxiety reaching a crescendo.

"He's stable," the doctor said with a calm, practiced tone. "The knife missed any vital organs. We've stitched him up, and with rest and some pain medication, he'll make a full recovery."

Emma let out a breath she hadn't realized she was holding. "Thank God," she whispered, pressing a hand to her chest.

Sarah nodded mutely, relief mixing with guilt that gnawed at the edges of her mind. "Can we see him?" she asked quietly.

The doctor nodded. "Just for a few minutes. He's still groggy, but he's asking for you."

Inside the room, Jake looked pale but alive. His eyes fluttered open as they entered, and he gave them a weak smile. "You look worse than me," he mumbled, his voice raspy.

Emma let out a nervous laugh as she stood by his side. "You're an idiot, you know that? Charging at him like that."

"Yeah, well, it worked, didn't it?" Jake replied, his lips twitching into a faint grin before wincing at the pain.

Sarah stayed near the door, her arms crossed tightly over her chest. "I'm so sorry, Jake," she said, trembling. "This is my fault. If I hadn't—"

"Stop," Jake interrupted, shaking his head as much as his stiff neck allowed. "None of this is your fault. That psycho was going to do something sooner or later. At least we're all still here."

Emma nodded, her eyes glistening. "You scared the hell out of us, Jake."

"Not as much as he scared me," Jake muttered, his attempt at humor falling flat. "But seriously, we'll figure this out. Together."

Later, at a quiet coffee shop, the three of them sat in a corner booth, the warm light from a nearby lamp doing little to ease the lingering chill in their bones. Jake sipped his coffee carefully, his movements slow and deliberate. Emma stirred her tea absentmindedly, the spoon clinking against the ceramic in a steady rhythm. Sarah sat silently, her hands wrapped tightly around her mug as if drawing strength from its warmth.

"You know," Jake said, breaking the silence, "for a guy who prides himself on being so smart, Caldwell didn't seem to think this through."

Emma frowned. "You think he didn't plan for this? The way he just showed up, like he knew we'd be too scared to act. That wasn't impulsive."

"He underestimated us," Jake replied firmly. "He thought he could intimidate us, but now the cops are involved, and they've seen what he's capable of."

Sarah's grip on her mug tightened. "It doesn't matter," she said softly, her voice heavy with dread. "He'll find a way. People like him... they don't just stop."

Jake leaned forward, his eyes serious. "We'll make sure he does, Sarah. He's not going to hurt anyone else."

Emma nodded, though her face betrayed her fear. "The police have him now. They won't just let him walk free."

Sarah stared out the window, watching the world outside carry on as if nothing had happened. People walked by with coffee cups in hand, cars honked faintly in the distance, and the hum of everyday life persisted. She wanted to believe the reassurances Jake and Emma offered, to feel like the worst was truly behind her, but Dr. Caldwell's words haunted her, chilling and deliberate: *This isn't our goodbye.*

Her voice broke the quiet, barely above a whisper. "I don't think it's over."

Jake shifted uncomfortably in his chair, glancing at Emma. For a moment, neither of them said anything. The silence spoke louder than words—they didn't think it was over either.

Finally, Jake leaned forward, his hands resting on the table. "You're right. It doesn't feel over. But we can't let him win, Sarah."

Emma nodded; her voice was soft but firm. "We can't let him control every part of our lives. He's already taken too much."

Sarah turned back to them, her gaze weary. "How do we even do that? How do we go back to normal after... everything?"

Jake rubbed the back of his neck. "I don't know if we go back to normal. But we have to try. Take it day by day. Go back to the things that make us... us."

Emma reached across the table, her hand a symbol of solidarity. "It's not going to be easy. We can't erase what happened. But we can't let fear dictate our lives. We must reclaim our lives."

She wanted to believe them, to imagine a life where she didn't look over her shoulder at every turn. A life where she didn't feel like a shadow was lurking, waiting to strike.

She nodded slowly. "We'll try. Even if it's hard, we'll try."

Jake raised his coffee cup in a small but significant gesture. "To living again. One step at a time. Together."

Emma gave him a weak but genuine smile. "One step at a time."

Sarah hesitated, then lifted her cup, clinking it softly against theirs. The warmth of the coffee wasn't enough to chase away the chill in her chest, but for the first time in days, it felt like a start.

Epilogue

Five Years Later

The soft hum of chatter and clinking glasses filled the upscale restaurant as Sarah, Emma, and Jake sat at a corner table, toasting to a milestone none of them ever thought they'd see: the fifth anniversary of Dr. Caldwell's arrest. The years since that terrifying night had been a mix of healing, rebuilding, and, for Sarah, rediscovering a sense of safety.

"Five years," Jake said, shaking his head as he raised his glass. "I still can't believe we made it through that shit."

"Not just made it," Emma added, smiling. "We fucking crushed it. Sarah's got her book deal, Jake's working for an insurance company, and I've got my dog and a plant that's only died twice. That's progress."

They all laughed, the kind of laughter that came quickly now, five years removed from the nightmare that had almost destroyed them.

Sarah raised her glass, her smile radiant. "I couldn't have done it without you two. I mean it. You saved my life."

Jake waved her off, though his face softened. "You would've done the same for us."

Emma smirked. "Let's not get all sappy now. We're here to celebrate. You're alive, that psycho is in prison where he belongs, and life is good."

Sarah nodded, letting herself relax. Life was good now. She'd spent years in therapy, rebuilding her confidence and learning to live without constantly looking over her shoulder. Dr. Caldwell had been convicted of stalking, attempted murder, and assault, thanks to the overwhelming evidence Sarah had gathered. He wasn't just behind bars—he was locked away for life.

"I'm just glad it's all behind me," Sarah said, her voice calm and steady. "No more fear. No more looking over my shoulder. It's done."

They clinked their glasses, smiling as they discussed plans. The past tense felt like a distant memory, finally at peace.

The waitress approached their table with the bill in hand as the meal wound down. She smiled politely as she set it down in front of Sarah, along with a folded piece of paper. "This is for you," the waitress said. "A man at the bar asked me to bring it over."

Sarah froze, her smile slipping. She stared at the note, her pulse quickening. Emma frowned. "What the fuck? Who?"

The waitress shrugged. "I didn't get a good look at him. He was wearing a hat. He left right after he gave me this."

Jake leaned forward, his eyes narrowing. "Sarah, don't open that."

But Sarah couldn't stop herself. Her hands trembled as she unfolded the note. The handwriting was neat and deliberate, the words simple but chilling:

"Hello, Sarah, it's been a while. You're looking good today." Her breath caught in her throat. The room seemed to tilt as the memories came rushing back—the notes, the photographs, the sound of his voice in the dark.

Emma grabbed the note, her face draining of color as she read it. "What the fuck is this?"

Jake stood up, his eyes scanning the restaurant. "Where the hell is this guy? Did you see him leave?" he demanded, turning to the waitress.

"No, I'm sorry," she said, her voice nervous. "He just... he left. Is everything okay?" Sarah didn't answer. Her hands were clenched tightly in her lap, her mind racing. It's not possible. He's in prison. He's locked up. He can't—

But the note said otherwise. Emma placed a hand on Sarah's arm, her voice firm.

"Sarah. He's locked away. This is just some sick fuck messing with you. It must be."

Sarah nodded slowly, but the knot of fear in her chest wouldn't loosen. The words on the note felt too familiar, too deliberate.

Jake sat back down, his expression dark. "We're calling the cops. Right now. They can track this asshole down."

As Emma dialed, Sarah forced herself to breathe. She looked around the restaurant, searching for something—someone—that didn't belong. But the room was full of happy, oblivious diners.

"Maybe it's a prank," she whispered, trying to convince herself. "Maybe someone heard the story and thought it'd be funny."

Jake shook his head. "That's not fucking funny. And it's not a coincidence. Whoever sent this—"

"Knows me," Sarah finished, her voice hollow.

The waitress returned, apologetic and confused. "I asked the bartender, but he didn't notice anything either. I'm so sorry."

"It's not your fault," Sarah said quickly, forcing a smile. As the waitress left, Sarah felt the note's weight. The handwriting was too perfect, reminding her of the same cursive she saw five years ago, evoking the same fear.

Emma hung up the phone. "The cops are sending someone over," she said. "They'll check the bar's security footage, but—"

"They won't find him," Sarah said quietly.

Jake frowned. "What are you talking about? They'll find him. And when they do, we'll—"

"It's him," Sarah whispered. Her voice was barely audible but cut through the room like a blade.

Jake and Emma exchanged uneasy glances. "Sarah, that's not possible," Emma said gently. "He's in prison. You know that."

Sarah looked down at the note, her hands trembling. “But what if he’s not?”

A cold, sinking feeling settled over her as she thought about the last five years. The safety she’d built and the life she’d rebuilt felt like a lie now.

Somehow, Dr. Caldwell had found a way back into her life. And this time, she wasn’t sure she’d survive him.

Driven by Madness

Chapter One

The Warning

The kitchen was quiet except for the slow, persistent drip of coffee into the pot. Cinnamon hung faintly in the air—a slight sweetness Julie insisted on, one that softened mornings for her but did nothing for him now. The light pouring through the window was golden and warm, the kind of light that belonged in another life, a simpler one. Not this one. Not this fragile, splintering mess he was living in.

Henry leaned against the counter, watching the dark liquid pool in the pot. His jaw was so tight it felt like his teeth might crack. He hated this—this quiet. It mocked him. Mocked the roiling storm inside his chest.

Behind him, Julie was humming. That damn song again, the one that spilled out whenever she was at ease, some old tune she never knew the name of. Her voice was soft, lilting, the sound that might've comforted him once. But now? It made his chest tighten. It felt like a noose tightening around his ribs.

"Hey," he called over his shoulder, his voice sharp, harsher than intended.

"Hmm?" she replied absently, her attention still glued to her phone.

"Are you even listening to me?" He could hear the edge in his tone, but he didn't care.

Julie looked up, startled. The sunlight caught her curls, framing her face in a way that made him ache. She smiled that soft, faraway smile that made his stomach churn. It was the kind of smile that said, *You're overreacting, Henry. Again.*

"What?" she asked lightly, setting her phone on the table like he interrupted her peace.

He turned, gripping the edge of the counter until his knuckles whitened. "The hitchhikers," he said, his voice low, simmering. "We need to talk about the goddamn hitchhikers."

Julie blinked at him, her smile twitching broader momentarily as if it were some joke. "Again?" she said with an airy laugh. "Henry, we've been over this."

"Yeah, again," he snapped, stepping closer to the table. His hands were clenched now, fingers digging into his palms. "Because you don't seem to get it. It's dangerous. You're putting yourself in danger every single time you stop for one of them."

Julie sighed, leaning back in her chair. She crossed her arms, her smile fading into that infuriatingly calm expression she always wore when she thought he was being ridiculous. "Henry, I don't just stop for anyone. I'm not stupid. I trust my gut."

"And your gut's supposed to stop a knife? A gun?" He gestured wildly, his voice rising. "You think you can *sense* who's a psycho and who's not? Jesus, Julie."

"Henry." Her tone was soft and measured. The way she said his name made his teeth grind. "You're paranoid."

He barked out a bitter laugh, dragging a hand down his face. "Paranoid? People are getting murdered out there, Julie. People who thought they were helping someone, doing the right thing. You think they didn't trust their gut, too?"

Julie tilted her head, her blue eyes softening like she was trying to calm a child. "Henry, not everyone is out to get you. Most of the people I stop for are just stranded. Normal people who need help."

"And it only takes one." His voice was sharper now, cutting through her calm like a blade. "One person who isn't fucking normal. One person to ruin everything." He stepped closer to her, his shadow falling over her. "You think the people on the news thought they'd be attacked? You think they didn't *trust* their instincts?"

She pressed her lips into a thin line, her arms tightening across her chest. "I've been doing this for years," she said softly. "And nothing bad has ever happened."

"*Yet.*" The word hung in the air like smoke. He saw the flicker of irritation cross her face, but she didn't respond. "You think you're invincible, Julie. But you're not. You can't control what other people do. And it scares the hell out of me."

For a moment, neither of them said anything. The hum of the coffee pot filled the silence. Then Julie leaned forward, her expression softening as she reached across the table and took his hand. Her touch was warm and steady. Familiar. "I know you worry about me," she said gently. "But I'm careful. I promise, Henry."

He stared at her, his jaw tight. She didn't get it. She *never* got it. Or maybe she did, and she didn't care. "Why?" he asked finally, his voice low, raw. "Why do you even do it? Why take the risk?"

Julie's expression shifted, something deep and unshakable settling into her eyes. "Because I couldn't live with myself if I didn't," she said. "If I saw someone who needed help and just drove by, pretending they didn't exist? That's not who I am."

Her words hit him like a blow. He wanted to argue, to make her see reason, but deep down, he knew he wouldn't win. Julie's heart was too big, too stubborn.

"Promise me you'll be extra careful," he said finally, his voice barely above a whisper.

"I always am." Her smile returned as she squeezed his hand, but the knot in Henry's stomach didn't loosen. If anything, it tightened as he watched her finish her coffee and grab her purse from the counter.

"I'll see you tonight," she said, kissing his cheek. Her lips were soft, fleeting. Too fleeting. This time, it felt different. It felt final.

Henry stood in the kitchen long after she'd left, staring at the empty coffee cup she'd left behind. Something was coming. He could feel it. The weight of it pressed down on him like a storm cloud, heavy and suffocating.

When Julie's car disappeared down the driveway, he had no idea it was the last time he'd see her alive.

Chapter Two

Blood on the Road

The scent of simmering tomato sauce filled the house, thick and cloying. It turned Henry's stomach. He stirred the pot absently, his eyes darting to the clock on the wall. 7:12 p.m. Julie was late.

She wasn't usually late. If she was running behind, she always called or texted—*stuck behind a tractor, be home soon :)*—the kind of message that made him roll his eyes and smile all at once. But tonight? Silence.

Henry wiped his hands on a dishrag and reached for his phone—no missed calls, no messages. He dialed her number, his fingers trembling slightly. It rang twice before going to voicemail.

"Hey, Jules," he said, forcing a casual tone. "Just checking in. You're running a little late. Give me a call, okay?" He hung up, his throat tight. The knot in his stomach was back, heavier than ever.

By 7:30, he was pacing the kitchen. The once-comforting creaks of the old house now felt like whispers of something wrong. At 7:45, he called her again. It went straight to voicemail. This time, there was no message. He slammed the phone down on the counter, his mind racing through every worst-case scenario.

Maybe her car broke down. Perhaps she got a flat tire. Maybe—

The shrill ring of his phone cut through his thoughts like a knife. He grabbed it, barely glancing at the screen before answering. "Julie?"

"This is Officer Davis with the state police." The voice was calm and professional. Too calm. "Am I speaking with Henry Turner?"

Henry's heart stopped. "Yes," he said, his voice barely above a whisper. "What's going on?"

"Your wife, Julie Turner... she's been found."

The words slammed into him, cold and sharp. "Found?" His voice cracked. "What do you mean, 'found'? Is she okay?"

The officer hesitated. "She was discovered on the side of Route 42. She appears to have been attacked. She's been transported to St. Andrew's Hospital."

Henry didn't even remember hanging up. His hands moved independently, grabbing his keys as he stumbled out the door. The drive to the hospital was a blur of headlights and darkness. He didn't think—couldn't think. All he could see was Julie lying on the side of the road, broken and bleeding, her hand reaching out for help.

When he finally arrived, the nurse directed him to Room 217. His legs felt like lead as he pushed open the door.

Julie was lying in the hospital bed, pale and bruised, her curls matted with dried blood. A clear oxygen mask covered her face, and an IV snaked into her arm. She looked impossibly small beneath the thin blanket.

"Julie," he whispered, sitting down beside her. He took her hand—it was cold, limp. "I'm here," he said, his voice breaking. "I'm here. You're safe now."

Her eyelids fluttered. For a moment, her glassy blue eyes locked onto his. "Henry," she rasped, her voice barely audible.

"I'm here," he repeated, squeezing her hand. "It's okay. You're going to be okay."

She swallowed hard, her lips trembling. "I'm sorry," she whispered.

"No," Henry said, shaking his head. "Don't say that. Don't apologize. ... tell me what happened. Who did this to you?"

Her chest rose and fell in shallow, uneven breaths. "A man... hitchhiker..." Her voice cracked, and Henry leaned closer, desperate to hear her.

"What did he look like?" he asked, his voice trembling. "Julie, what did he look like?"

"Brown hair... scar... left cheek..." Her breathing grew more labored, her eyes fluttering shut.

"Julie? Julie, stay with me!" The heart monitor began to beep erratically. "No, no, no! Don't go! Please don't go!"

The monitor flatlined. The doctors burst in, but Henry already knew. She was gone.

Chapter Three

Descent into Darkness

The days after Julie's death blurred into a haze of empty hours and sleepless nights. The house felt wrong—too quiet, too full of her absence. It smelled like her still, lavender and cinnamon clinging stubbornly to the air. The ghost of her laugh haunted every room, the echo of her presence.

The police were kind but useless. Sympathetic, professional, but detached. Their words were carefully chosen, designed to offer comfort without promises. *"We'll do everything we can."* But Henry saw the truth in their eyes. Julie wasn't their priority. She was just another file on their desk, another case that might never be solved.

He wanted to scream at them, to grab their collars and shake them until they understood—Julie wasn't just a case. She was *everything.* And now she was gone.

Weeks passed, and the world moved on. But Henry didn't. He couldn't. The rage clawed at him day and night, a gnawing, insatiable thing that left no room for grief. He saw her everywhere—in the curve of the coffee cup she used to drink from, in the way the sunlight hit the kitchen window. But the one place he saw her most vividly was in his dreams. Her broken body was on the side of the road. She whispered words. *Brown hair. Scar. Left cheek.*

The police didn't seem to care about those words. But Henry did. The first time he went to Route 42, he wasn't sure what he was looking for. He parked on the shoulder where she'd been found, the headlights casting long, ghostly shadows on the empty road. The air was cold and damp, the chill that crept into your bones and stayed there.

He sat in his car, staring into the darkness, imagining her last moments. The hitchhiker. The man with the scar. Had he been smiling when she stopped for him? Did he look harmless? Trustworthy? Had he thanked her before he tore her life apart?

Henry's hands tightened on the steering wheel. His knuckles turned white, his nails digging into his palms. He wanted to scream. He wanted to punch something until his fists bled. But instead, he waited. And watched.

Hours passed. The road remained empty. Finally, he turned the car around and drove home. But something had shifted in him that night. The anger that had been festering inside him had found a purpose.

Chapter Four

The Factory

It started small—a chance sighting. A hitchhiker standing on the side of the road, their thumb outstretched, their silhouette barely visible in the dim glow of the moonlight. Henry slowed his car, his heart pounding. He didn't know why he stopped. Maybe it was curiosity. Perhaps it was something darker.

The man climbed into the passenger seat with a grateful smile. "Thanks, man. I've been walking for hours. You're a lifesaver."

Henry didn't answer. He just nodded, his eyes fixed on the road. His mind was racing, a thousand thoughts colliding at once. This wasn't the man with the scar. He knew that. But picking up a hitchhiker felt like taking control, like reclaiming some small piece of what had been stolen from him.

"You don't talk much, huh?" the man said, chuckling nervously. "That's cool. I'll enjoy the ride."

Henry's fingers twitched on the steering wheel. His gaze flicked to the center console, where the taser was hidden beneath an old map. He hadn't planned this. He didn't even know what he was going to do. But the weight of the taser called to him a dark temptation he couldn't ignore.

When he finally stopped the car, the man looked confused. "Why are we—"

Henry didn't let him finish. He lunged for the taser, pressing it into the man's side and pulling the trigger. The man convulsed, his body jerking violently before slumping against the seat, unconscious.

The factory was an old, abandoned relic on the edge of town. Henry had driven past it a hundred times before, never giving it a second thought. Now, as he dragged the unconscious man through the broken front doors, it felt like destiny.

The air inside was thick with the smell of rust and decay. Machinery long forgotten loomed in the shadows, its jagged edges like the bones of some long-dead beast. Henry tied the man to a chair with a rope length, his movements steady and methodical. His hands didn't tremble. He didn't hesitate. He grabbed a monkey wrench left behind and placed it by the chair.

When the man woke, his groggy confusion quickly turned to panic. "What the fuck is this? Let me go, man!"

Henry stepped closer, holding up the photo of Julie. "Do you know her?" he asked, his voice low and cold.

The man's eyes darted to the photo, then back to Henry. "No, I don't know her! I swear! What the fuck is this?"

"You're lying," Henry said, his voice sharp. "You all lie." He grabbed the wrench. The first blow was almost hesitant. Almost. But when the man screamed, when the sound of bone cracking echoed through the factory, something inside Henry shifted. The hesitation was gone. The rage took over. Every swing of the wrench, every scream, felt like a release. Like justice.

When it was over, the man was slumped in the chair, his body broken and lifeless. Henry stared at him long, waiting for the guilt to come. But it didn't. There was only a cold, hollow satisfaction.

This wasn't the man who killed Julie. But it didn't matter. They were all the same.

Chapter Five

The Encounter

Henry became a regular on Route 42. He learned to spot them—the hitchhikers. The ones who looked like they didn't belong. He kept his car clean, his demeanor calm. He practiced smiling, though it never quite reached his eyes. He became good at hiding the darkness inside him.

Thirteen. That was the number. Thirteen people who thought they were getting a lucky break. Thirteen people who never made it to their destination. Henry didn't know about them. They were just shadows, ghosts that faded into the background of his mind. Until the night he saw him.

The scar caught the light as the man stepped onto the shoulder of the road, his thumb outstretched, a battered duffel bag slung over his shoulder. Henry's heart raced, his hands tightening on the wheel. Brown hair. Scar. Left cheek.

It was him.

He slowed the car, his pulse thundering in his ears. The man jogged to the passenger side and leaned down to the window. "Hey, thanks for stopping."

Henry forced a smile. "Get in."

As the man climbed into the car, Henry's mind churned. This was it. This was the moment he'd been waiting for. But as the factory loomed in the distance, a new thought crept into his mind.

What if he was wrong? It would be another sorry excuse for a life gone from this world if he were. That made him smile.

The factory loomed ahead, a jagged silhouette against the night sky. Henry's heart thundered in his chest, but his hands were steady on the wheel. The man with the scar sat beside him, oblivious, leaning back in the seat as if this was just another ride.

"So," the man said, his voice casual, "you live around here?"

Henry didn't answer immediately. He glanced at the man out of the corner of his eye, studying the scar on his cheek, the roughness of his hands, and the slight smirk that tugged at his lips. Was it him? Could it be him?

"I live close," Henry said finally, his tone clipped. He didn't want to say more. I didn't want to give this man anything.

The scarred man shifted in his seat, his eyes flicking toward the darkness outside the window. "Not much out here, is there? Are you sure this is the quickest way to town?"

"It is," Henry said flatly.

The man seemed to sense the shift in tone. He turned to Henry, his expression sharpening. "You're acting weird, man. Everything okay?"

Henry forced a tight smile. "Everything's fine."

When they reached the factory, Henry pulled the car to a stop. The scarred man frowned, leaning forward to peer at the crumbling building. "This doesn't look like a shortcut."

"It is," Henry said, his voice cold. He reached for the taser in the center console, his fingers brushing the smooth plastic. "Get out."

The man turned to him, suspicion darkening his face. "What the fuck are you—"

Henry didn't give him a chance to finish. He lunged, jamming the taser into the man's side and pulling the trigger. The man was soon unconscious like the rest of them.

Henry sat back, his chest heaving. His hands were trembling now, but he ignored the sensation. He reached over and unbuckled the man's seatbelt, dragging his limp body out of the car and toward the factory.

Chapter Six

Blood and Bones

The man woke to pain. His wrists and ankles were bound to the chair, the ropes digging into his skin. The flickering flashlight in the corner cast long, jagged shadows on the walls, making the room feel alive and predatory.

Henry stood a few feet away, watching him with cold, unblinking eyes. In his hand was the photo of Julie, her smile frozen in time, a cruel reminder of everything he'd lost.

"Do you know her?" Henry asked, his voice low, almost a growl.

The man squinted at the photo, his brow furrowing. "What... what is this?" he croaked. "Who the fuck are you?"

Henry stepped closer, holding the photo before the man's face. "Do you know her?" he repeated, his voice sharper now.

The man shook his head, his eyes wide with confusion and fear. "No, I don't know her! I don't know what this is about, but you've got the wrong guy!"

Henry's jaw tightened. He grabbed the man by the collar, pulling him forward until their faces were inches apart. "Brown hair. The scar on your left cheek. She described you before she died."

The man's eyes darted away, panic flashing across his face. "Look, I've picked up rides before. Maybe I saw her, I don't know! But I didn't kill anyone! I swear to God, I didn't kill her!"

Henry's hand shot out, slamming the photo to the ground with enough force to rattle the room. His eyes burned with unrelenting rage as he roared, "You're fucking lying! You left her on the side of the road like she was trash! Tell me the truth before I tear it out of you!"

The man flinched, his voice breaking as he shouted, "I *am* telling the truth!"

Henry's lips twisted into a grim, humorless smile. "Funny. You don't sound very convincing." His hand closed around the rusted wrench on the table—a heavy, ugly thing coated with grime.

Without warning, he swung. The wrench connected with the man's leg with a sickening crunch, and the sound of bone snapping echoed like a gunshot. The man let out a scream so raw it could strip paint off the walls. His leg bent at an angle nature never intended, and Henry tilted his head, staring at the grotesque twist.

"Would you look at that," Henry muttered, almost amused. "Guess you're not running anywhere, huh?"

"Fuck! Fuck!" the man shrieked, his hands gripping the chair as he nearly toppled backward.

Henry caught the chair and slammed it back upright, the motion violent enough to make the man's teeth clack together. "Ah, ah," Henry said, wagging a finger. "We're not done yet. You're not passing out on me, either. Not until I get some fucking answers."

"Jesus Christ, man!" the man gasped, sweat pouring down his face.

"Jesus isn't here," Henry snapped. "It's just you, me, and the truth you seem real fucking hesitant to share. So let's try this again, shall we?" He leaned in close, his breath hot and acrid against the man's ear.

"Do. You. Fucking. Know. Her?" Each word dripped with venom. "What did you do to her? And before you even *think* about lying to me again..." He tapped the wrench lightly against the man's good leg. "Well, you're already halfway to a wheelchair, so let's see how lucky you're feeling tonight."

The man whimpered, his eyes darting wildly around the room like salvation might come bursting through the walls. It wouldn't.

"You're fucking insane," the man croaked.

Henry smirked a cold, hollow thing. "Yeah. I get that a lot. Now talk."

"I didn't hurt her! I just... I just took her car and left! I didn't know she'd... I didn't know she was hurt!"

Henry froze, the man's words slicing through his rage like a blade. He stared at him, his chest heaving, his mind racing.

I just took her car and left. Henry repeated in his mind.

The words didn't fit. They didn't match the narrative he'd built in his head. But they didn't absolve this man, either.

"Because it's the truth!" the man cried. "I stole her car, okay? I'm a piece of shit, but I didn't kill her! She was alive when I left! You have to believe me!"

Henry's hand twitched at his side, his knuckles white around the wrench's handle. His vision tunneled the man's voice, a distant echo as the rage inside him boiled over.

"Alive?" Henry growled, his voice low, almost disbelieving. "You left her. Alone. And you want me to believe she was fine?" "Why should I believe you?" Henry said, his voice trembling, a dangerous edge creeping in. "Why should I believe anything you fucking say?"

"I swear!" the man sobbed, shaking his head desperately. "I swear on my life, I didn't hurt her! Please, man! Please don't—"

The wrench came down with a sickening crack, cutting off the man's words. His scream tore through the air, raw and panicked, as Henry's shadow loomed over him like a specter of death.

"No!" the man screamed, his voice breaking. "Please! I'm telling the truth! Don't do this! Please, don't—"

Another blow. And another.

"Don't?" Henry snarled, his voice filled with venom. "You're asking *me* for mercy? After what you did to her?"

The man's pleas devolved into incoherent sobbing as Henry swung again, the wrench breaking bone, shattering flesh. Each strike was met with a sickening wet sound, and soon, the man's screams faded to pitiful gurgles.

"Tell me the truth!" Henry roared, his voice echoing through the factory as the wrench fell again. "Tell me why you left her! Why did you leave her to die!"

But the man was beyond answering now. His face was no longer a face, just a mangled mess of blood and bone, his body limp, twitching faintly with the last remnants of life.

Henry stood there, chest heaving, the bloodied wrench hanging from his trembling hand. He stared down at the ruined corpse, his ears ringing in the deafening silence.

He staggered back, dropping the wrench with a metallic clang. For a moment, he swayed, lightheaded from exhaustion. His legs threatened to buckle, but he forced himself to move.

Without a word, he crouched down and began scraping up what was left of the man, scooping the mess into a dented trash can nearby. The motions felt mechanical, almost dreamlike as if someone else were guiding his hands. He tossed in the chunks, the gore, the blood-soaked scraps of what was once a human being. The rest of him, the unrecognizable remnants on the floor, he left behind.

Henry rose unsteadily to his feet, wiping his bloody hands on his shirt. He didn't look back as he walked out of the factory, the air thick with the stench of death.

The cold night greeted him, the wind biting his skin, but Henry barely noticed. His thoughts were a blur, his hands still shaking.

Would he return to the factory?

The thought hung in the air, unanswered. But deep down, he already knew.

Epilogue

The Cycle

The factory stood silent and empty, its jagged walls a monument to the horrors that had unfolded there. The faint smell of oil and rust lingered in the air, mingling with the ghostly echoes of screams long since silenced. Shattered glass and discarded tools littered the floor, mute witnesses to the violence that had consumed the space. The dim light filtering through the broken windows gave the place an eerie, lifeless glow. It was as though the building held its breath, waiting for someone to uncover its secrets.

The police would find it eventually. They always did. The bodies buried in the woods behind the factory would tell a grim tale—the remains of lives cut short, victims of a man consumed by grief and rage. They would piece together the story, or at least what little they could. Forensic evidence would lead them to the tools Henry had used, the makeshift graveyard he had created. But the truth? The whole, unvarnished truth of what had driven him to such madness? That would remain buried with him, hidden in the dark corners of his shattered mind.

Henry was already gone. No one knew where, and perhaps no one ever would. He had vanished like a ghost, leaving behind only questions and carnage. Some might have called him a monster, others a man broken by tragedy. But whatever he had become, he was no longer bound by the laws of men. He was something else now, something untethered and dangerous.

The roads stretched endlessly before him, dark and empty, illuminated only by the moon's pale glow. His car—the same one Julie had loved, with its worn seats and faintly rattling engine—carried him forward, mile after mile. He hadn't planned where he was going. He just drove, the engine's hum a dull backdrop to the storm raging in his head.

On another desolate stretch of highway, another hitchhiker waited for a ride—a man with tired eyes and a story too well-rehearsed. Henry's grip on the wheel tightened as he thought about them. The ones who preyed on the vulnerable. The ones who turned trust into tragedy. The cycle of violence would continue, as it always had.

But now, there was someone new in the game. A man who had lost everything and found a purpose in the ashes of his old life. He wasn't a savior, and he wasn't a hero. He was a shadow, a consequence, a reckoning. The hitchhikers wouldn't see him coming until it was too late. And when they did, they would know what it felt like to face the weight of their sins.

The factory would remain a rotting husk filled with the whispers of the past. The woods would grow over the graves, hiding the evidence of what had been. And the highways? They would carry Henry forward wherever his need for vengeance and justice would take him next.

Somewhere in the distance, a signpost flashed by, but Henry didn't read it. It didn't matter. He wasn't looking for a destination. He was looking for the next shadow to extinguish. The cycle of violence continued, but now, so did he.

The Ice Cream Incident

Chapter One

Content Creator Life

Rachel slouched in her chair, squinting at her laptop screen as she painstakingly fine tuned her latest YouTube masterpiece. Editing was never her favorite part, but the thought of hitting "upload" and watching the comments roll in always made it worth the grind.

"Okay, final touch… and done!" she declared to no one, slamming her laptop shut with the flair of a Hollywood hacker. Of course, this heroic gesture did nothing to speed up the upload, but it felt satisfying.

Her stomach growled loud enough to startle her cat, Mittens, who shot her a judgmental look from the windowsill. "Alright, food it is," Rachel muttered as she pushed herself up from the chair. She opened the fridge with a dramatic flourish, hoping for inspiration, but found only expired milk, a single limp pickle, and half a tub of hummus.

"Why am I like this," she groaned, shutting the fridge and yanking open the freezer. Salvation revealed itself in the form of a frozen pizza and what looked suspiciously like a container of ice cream. She raised the pizza box high above her head. "Bless past me for buying this," she announced, holding it like Simba in The Lion King.

Minutes later the pizza was in the oven, soda fizzed into a glass, and Rachel dropped back into her chair in what she liked to call her editing uniform. Baggy sweatpants and an old t shirt clung to her, the kind of clothes that had survived far too many late nights. Comfort over style, always.

While the pizza cooked, she checked the comments on her last video. Most were the usual kind words. "Nice job, Rachel." "Love your energy." "This made my day." She beamed, her confidence puffing up just enough to erase some of the boredom of editing. Then came that one sour note. "You're funny, but your laugh is kind of annoying."

Rachel narrowed her eyes. "Thanks for the unsolicited critique, Karen," she muttered. She refused to let one salty comment sour her vibe.

The oven timer dinged. She hurried to the kitchen, pulled the pizza out, and admired it like a priceless work of art. As it cooled, she poured herself another soda, the fizzing sound as satisfying as a game victory screen.

Balancing her plate and drink, she logged into Twitch. Her favorite streamer, Hailbat22, was live, and Rachel's heart lifted. Not only was Hailbat22 her role model, funny and fearless, but Rachel also served as a moderator on her channel. Wielding the banhammer against trolls was one of her guilty pleasures.

She typed a quick "Hi!" into chat. Hailbat22's voice rang out, "Rachel's here! What's up, mod queen?" Rachel smiled, but decided to mostly lurk today. Pizza grease and keyboards did not mix.

The chat scrolled with its usual chaos, a mix of wholesome fans and bizarre comments. One person swore they were typing with their toes, another declared eternal love. Rachel scanned for troublemakers, but Hailbat22 was on point. When someone typed "You look like you smell like cheese," she clapped back instantly. "If I smelled like cheese, I'd be gouda. Get it? Goo da?"

Rachel snorted mid sip and nearly sprayed soda across the table. "Oh my god," she laughed, shaking her head.

By the time the stream wound down, the pizza was gone, the soda was flat, and Mittens was asleep in the same spot as before. Rachel brushed crumbs off her sweats and stretched. The day had been cozy, full of small joys and the kind of chaotic energy only the internet could provide.

"Alright, Rachel," she said, grinning at her reflection in the darkened laptop screen. "Let's make something amazing tomorrow."

She didn't know it yet, but tomorrow's vlog would be unlike anything she had ever recorded.

Chapter Two

Dressing for the Heat

Rachel shut her laptop with a satisfied sigh. Pizza demolished, soda drained, and Hailbat22's stream still buzzing in her head, she felt restless. The night had been fun, but the same four walls were starting to feel like a cage.

She glanced at her tripod leaning by the door and smirked. "Alright, Rachel, enough being a gremlin. Time to get some real footage."

Kicking off her slippers, she shuffled to the closet and pulled the door open. Her reflection in the mirror reminded her she was still in her editing uniform: baggy sweats and a stretched out shirt with a faded cartoon print. She laughed at herself. "Yeah, not exactly vlog worthy."

After rifling through the chaos of her closet, she found it. Her favorite purple sundress. She hadn't worn it in weeks, maybe months, but the moment she slipped it on, the mood shifted. Pairing it with sandals and a wide brimmed hat, she studied herself in the mirror.

"Not too bad, Rachel," she said with mock confidence. "You might actually pass for someone who has their life together."

Mittens, still sprawled across the windowsill, flicked his tail as if to disagree.

She tossed essentials into her tote bag: phone, tripod, wallet, water bottle, and the portable charger she never trusted herself to leave behind. She paused at the freezer for a moment, staring at the half melted ice cream tub, then shook her head. "Don't tempt me. We're saving the ice cream bit for outside."

Slinging the bag over her shoulder, Rachel grabbed her sunglasses and struck a dramatic pose in the hallway mirror. "Okay, park vlog, here we come."

She gave Mittens one last glance. "Guard the kingdom while I'm gone."

He yawned in reply.

With that, she stepped outside, pulling the door shut behind her. The air felt warm against her skin, the kind of evening that promised summer vibes. Rachel adjusted her hat, already rehearsing silly one liners for her vlog.

She had no idea what was waiting for her just a few blocks away.

Chapter Three

A Walk to Remember

Rachel adjusted her tote bag as she stepped out of her apartment, the warm evening air brushing her skin. She tilted her camera toward herself, hitting record with a grin.

"Alright, internet," she announced, "your girl has traded sweats for a sundress. Mark your calendars. This is historic."

She walked down the block, narrating like a travel show host. "On your left, we have the world famous corner of 5th and Maple, known for its... well, stop signs." She zoomed in dramatically, then spun the camera back toward her face. "Breathtaking, I know."

Mittens wasn't there to roll his eyes, but Rachel imagined him doing it anyway.

By the time she reached the park, the chatter of families and the squeals of children filled the air. The smell of grilled hot dogs drifted from somewhere nearby. Rachel swung her camera around to capture the scene. "And here we have the majestic playground, populated by wild creatures known as toddlers."

That was when she heard it—the familiar jingle of an ice cream truck. She froze mid sentence, her eyes lighting up.

"Hold up. Is that...?" She panned the camera toward the jingling music. Sure enough, the truck was parked by the curb, a small line forming in front of it.

Rachel laughed. "Okay, vlog pivot. Forget nature footage. Ice cream is clearly the main event."

She joined the line, humming along to the tinny tune blasting from the truck. The person behind her coughed loudly, but she ignored it, scrolling through flavor options in her head like she was choosing her final meal.

When it was her turn, she ordered without hesitation. "One triple scoop of Rocky Road, please."

Cone in hand, she turned to find a place to sit. That was when she felt the tap on her shoulder.

She spun around and came face to face with a man from the line. His eyes were too wide, his grin a little too fixed. Rachel opened her mouth to say something, but before she could, he snatched her cone, smashed it onto his forehead, and bellowed, "I'm a rhino!"

For a heartbeat, Rachel froze, her brain refusing to process what just happened. Then the man sprinted off, dripping Rocky Road down his face as if nothing were out of the ordinary.

The silence lasted only a second before Rachel burst into laughter. "Well. That's new."

Pulling out her phone, she hit record again, her voice shaking with giggles. "So, guys, update. I just lost my ice cream to a human rhino impersonator. Ten out of ten for commitment. Zero out of ten for manners."

Still laughing, she brushed melted ice cream from her sundress and shook her head. "Guess that's today's vlog sorted."

She had no idea how right she was.

Chapter Four

Viral Momentum

By the time Rachel made it back to her apartment, the adrenaline had finally worn off, leaving behind pure disbelief. She set her tripod on the counter, replaying the moment in her head. The man's voice, the dripping ice cream, the absolute absurdity of it all—it was too good not to share.

She loaded the footage onto her computer and began editing, unable to stop herself from laughing every few minutes. She slowed the moment he yelled "I'm a rhino," added dramatic zooms, and even threw in a stock sound effect of a trumpet.

"Perfect," she said, wiping a tear from her eye.

She titled the vlog *"Ice Cream Rhino Attack!"* and hit upload, sharing it across every social media platform she had. Then she sat back with a fresh soda, waiting.

The response was immediate. Comments flooded in within minutes.

- *"This made my day!"*
- *"Only you, Rachel, could attract a rhino in the park!"*
- *"I can't stop laughing, please do more content like this!"*

Her subscriber count ticked upward like a slot machine jackpot.

Rachel grinned, leaning back in her chair. "Okay, so losing my ice cream wasn't a tragedy after all."

But the night wasn't done with her.

While scrolling through Twitter mentions, she saw her clip had already been reposted by meme accounts. One caption read, *"When life hits you like a charging rhino."* Another had gif'd the forehead smash in an endless loop.

Her phone buzzed with a DM notification. To her shock, it was from Hailbat22 herself.

"Rachel. I just watched your vlog. You are officially my hero. Also, I'm never eating Rocky Road again."

Rachel laughed so hard she nearly choked on her soda.

She flipped on her camera again for a follow up vlog, her grin unstoppable. "Moral of the story, folks—life is unpredictable. Sometimes you get pizza. Sometimes you get a rhino. And if you're lucky, you get both."

Mittens meowed from the windowsill, unimpressed as ever.

Rachel gave him a mock salute. "Don't worry, buddy. Next time, I'm buying two cones."

The Crimson Veil

Chapter One

The Arivial

Ash Hollow wasn't the kind of town where anything exciting happened. The biggest event of the year was the annual pie-eating contest at the fall festival, and even that usually ended in mild disappointment and mild heartburn. It was where people knew your name, your dog's name, and probably the last three things you bought at the grocery store. But that October morning, the town woke up to something it couldn't explain—and couldn't handle.

It started just before sunrise. The mist rolled in from the hills like a wave of blood. Thick, red, and wrong. It hugged the ground, moving with almost liquid grace, slithering into every alley, every yard, every corner of Ash Hollow like it was searching for something. Or someone.

Sheriff Hank Reilly saw it first. He was parked outside the gas station, sipping from a thermos of coffee that tasted like burnt motor oil, watching as the raccoons finished a late-night raid on the dumpster. They always put on a good show, little bastards. But then the red mist crept in, cutting across the road like a slow-moving tide.

Hank squinted, leaning forward in his seat. "The fuck is this now?"

At first, he thought it might've been smoke from one of the farms on Ridge Road—Frank Mathers always managed to set something on fire this time of year. But there was no smell of smoke. No ash. The air didn't even feel right. It felt... heavy. Metallic. Like the smell of pennies mixed with something Hank couldn't quite place.

He reached for the radio. "Dispatch, this is Reilly. Are you seeing this shit? Over."

Silence.

"Darla, come on. You fall asleep at the desk again?"

Static.

Hank frowned, tapping the radio like that was going to fix it. "Goddamn thing."

The mist was thicker now, rolling up the main road like a carpet of red death. It swallowed streetlights, phone poles, everything. One minute, you could see the Waffle Shack sign up ahead, and the next, gone. Hank tried to shake off the unease settling in his gut. He didn't get paid enough to worry about weird weather. That was somebody else's problem.

Still, when the cruiser radio failed him for the third time, Hank decided to drive up Main Street and look closer. The mist wrapped around the car like a living thing, curling up the windows and sliding across the hood. He turned on the high beams, but they barely cut through it. It was like trying to shine a flashlight through a bucket of blood.

"What the actual fuck is this?" Hank muttered, gripping the steering wheel tighter. He rolled the window down an inch—just enough to get a better look—and immediately gagged. The air was sharp, cold, and coppery, like the inside of a slaughterhouse.

A shape loomed ahead—a figure barely visible through the red haze. Hank slowed the cruiser, squinting. Someone was standing in the middle of the road, their silhouette swaying back and forth like a drunk on a bender.

"Christ," Hank muttered, pulling to a stop. He grabbed his flashlight and stepped out of the car. The air hit him like a punch to the gut, that metallic tang sticking to the back of his throat. He gagged, wiping his mouth with his sleeve, and called out, "Hey! You, okay? What the hell are you doing out here?"

No response. The figure kept swaying.

"Goddammit," Hank muttered, clicking on his flashlight. The beam cut through the mist, revealing a man in a flannel shirt and work boots. His face was slack and pale, his eyes unfocused. Hank recognized him immediately.

"Tom Heller?" he called, stepping closer. "You drunk again? Jesus, Martha's going to kill you."

Tom didn't answer. His lips twitched, like he was trying to say something but couldn't get the words out. Then Hank noticed the wrench in Tom's hand, slick with something dark that wasn't oil. His stomach twisted.

"Tom," Hank said, his voice lower now, more cautious. "What's going on? You hurt?"

Tom's head jerked up at the sound of Hank's voice, and for a second, their eyes met. Tom's pupils were blown wide, his gaze wild and glassy, like he saw something Hank couldn't. And then he smiled. It wasn't a friendly smile—it was the kind of grin you'd see on a guy who's just decided to burn down his own house for the insurance money. It was all wrong.

"Tom?" Hank asked again, taking a step back. "You with me, buddy?"

Without warning, Tom lunged. Hank barely had time to react. The wrench swung at his head, and he ducked just in time, the metal whistling past his ear. "What the fuck, Tom?!" he yelled, stumbling back. "Have you lost your goddamn mind?"

Tom didn't answer. He swung again, this time catching Hank on the arm. Pain shot up his shoulder, and he hissed, grabbing for his gun. "I don't want to do this, Tom!" Hank shouted. "You need to calm the fuck down right now!"

But Tom wasn't listening. He was snarling now, his teeth bared like a goddamn animal. Hank had no choice. He pulled the trigger. The shot echoed through the mist, and Tom crumpled to the ground, the wrench slipping from his hand.

Hank stood there, panting, his gun still raised. His ears rang from the shot, but he could still hear the mist. It was moving, curling around Tom's body like it was... feeding.

"What in the actual fuck is happening?" Hank muttered, lowering his gun. His arm throbbed where Tom had hit him, but the pain barely registered. All he could do was stare at the mist as it seemed to thicken, pulsing faintly like it had a heartbeat.

He stumbled back to the cruiser, slamming the door shut behind him. His hand trembled as he reached for the radio. "Dispatch, this is Reilly. We've got... something going on here. Something bad. I need backup. I need help. Now."

Static.

"Goddammit!" He slammed his fist against the dashboard. The mist was creeping up the windshield, turning the world outside into a swirling sea of red. For the first time in his life, Hank Reilly was afraid—not of a drunk with a wrench, not of some bullshit storm. He was worried because he didn't know what was happening, and he didn't know how to stop it.

And somewhere deep in the mist, he swore he could hear it breathing.

Chapter Two

The First Signs

The mist didn't stop. It didn't thin out or burn off with the morning sun like a regular fog. It only got thicker, clinging to Ash Hollow like it was trying to smother the town. By mid-morning, the red haze had swallowed everything—the streets, the fields, even the top of the water tower. The only thing anyone could see was that oppressive red glow.

And that's when people started to lose their shit.

Martha Keller had spent most of her sixty-seven years in Ash Hollow and wasn't about to let some creepy fog mess with her routine. She'd woken up at dawn, brewed her coffee, and gone out onto her porch in her pink bathrobe, just like she always did. The mist was weird, but the world didn't stop turning because the weather got spooky.

"Tom!" she called over her shoulder into the house. "You see this? Looks like someone spilled red paint all over the damn sky!"

No response.

"Tom?"

Martha frowned and set her coffee down on the railing. She shuffled back into the house, her slippers making a soft slap-slap on the hardwood. She found Tom in the kitchen, standing perfectly still in front of the sink. His hands were wet, but he wasn't washing dishes. He wasn't doing anything. Just... standing there, staring at the wall.

"Tom, what the hell are you doing?" Martha asked, irritation creeping into her voice.

Tom didn't answer.

Martha rolled her eyes. "You deaf now, too? I said—"

Then she saw the knife in his hand. A long butcher knife dripping water onto the floor. Martha's heart skipped a beat. "Tom?"

He turned to her slowly, like a rusty hinge creaking open. His eyes were wide, glassy, and unblinking, and his lips were twisted into the strangest smile she'd ever seen. A grin that didn't belong on her husband's face. It was like he was wearing it as if it didn't fit.

"Tom, you're scaring me," she said, her voice shaky. "Put the knife down, okay? Just... put it down."

Tom tilted his head, his grin widening. "I didn't mean to leave him," he whispered, his voice strange and guttural. "But he's here now."

"What the hell are you talking about? Leave who?"

He didn't answer. He just raised the knife and lunged at her.

Martha screamed and scrambled backward, her slipper catching on the edge of the carpet. She fell hard, the wind knocked out of her, and Tom was on her before she could get up. His face was inches from hers, his grin stretching so wide it looked like it might split his cheeks open.

"You can't run," he whispered, his breath hot and rancid against her skin. "It's already inside you."

Martha did the only thing she could think of. She grabbed the hot coffee mug from the table and smashed it into Tom's face. The ceramic shattered, and he howled, reeling backward. Martha didn't wait. She scrambled to her feet and bolted out the front door, screaming at the top of her lungs.

"Help! Somebody, help me!"

The mist swallowed her cries.

At Bert's Diner, things weren't much better. By 9:00 AM, the place was packed with the usual morning crowd—truckers, retirees, and a couple of teenagers skipping school. The red mist outside had everyone on edge, but Bert had kept the coffee flowing and the bacon sizzling, cracking jokes to keep things light.

"It's just fog," he said, slapping a plate of pancakes onto the counter. "Weird fog, sure, but this town's been weird since the seventies. Remember that UFO thing? Same shit, different day."

"Yeah, well," muttered Eric, the plumber, "the UFOs didn't make me feel like I'm going to vomit my guts out. This air tastes like a mouthful of pennies."

"Quit bitching and eat your pancakes," Bert shot back. "You'll live."

The bell over the door jingled, and Bert turned to see Sadie McCall, the high school art teacher, stumble inside. Her hair was messy, and her face was pale and sweaty, like she'd just run a marathon. She wasn't wearing her usual calm, bohemian smile. Instead, her eyes darted around the diner, wide and frantic.

"Sadie?" Bert said, setting down his spatula. "Are you alright, hon?"

Sadie didn't answer. She was muttering under her breath, something too soft to hear. Then she started laughing. It wasn't a usual laugh—it was high and shrill, bubbling out of her like she didn't control it.

"Uh... Sadie?" Bert stepped around the counter, his brow furrowing. "What's so funny?"

Sadie's laughter cut off like a switch had been flipped. She looked at him, her eyes suddenly dead serious. "They're here," she whispered.

Bert blinked. "What?"

"They're here," she said again, louder this time. Then she grabbed a steak knife off the nearest table and lunged at Eric, the plumber.

Chaos erupted.

Eric screamed as Sadie drove the knife into his shoulder, her face twisted with manic glee. People scrambled out of their seats, shouting and shoving as they tried to escape. Bert grabbed a skillet from the counter and swung it as hard as he could, catching Sadie in the side of the head. She went down, the knife clattering to the floor.

"Jesus fucking Christ!" Bert yelled, breathing hard. "What the hell is going on?"

Sadie lay on the floor, twitching and muttering to herself. The other customers stared at her, their faces pale with shock.

"We need to call the sheriff," someone said.

"Good luck with that," Bert muttered, wiping sweat from his brow. "Radio's been out all morning. Phones, too."

"So, what do we do?" another voice asked, panicked. "We can't just sit here!"

Bert stared down at Sadie, his grip tightening on the skillet. She was smiling again, her lips stained with blood.

"They're coming," she whispered.

And then the lights flickered and went out.

By midday, the mist had taken over the entire town. It wasn't just a weather phenomenon anymore—it was alive. It crawled through windows, seeped under doors, and pressed against people's minds like it was trying to crack them open. And for many, it succeeded.

Teachers turned on each other at the school, desks, and chairs flying in a bloody frenzy. At the grocery store, a cashier beat a customer to death with a can of soup. People were hearing voices and seeing things that weren't there. Shadows moved at the edges of their vision, and whispers filled their ears.

Still shaken from his encounter with Tom Heller, Sheriff Hank Reilly tried to regain some semblance of order. He drove through the mist-covered streets, his cruiser's siren wailing, but every call for help led to another horror show.

On Elm Street, he found the Jenkins family in their driveway. The father was standing over his wife's body with a tire iron, his face blank and emotionless. Their two kids were huddled in the corner of the garage, crying. When Hank approached, the father turned and lunged at him without a word.

Hank had no choice. He shot him.

It was the third person he'd killed that day, and it wasn't getting any easier.

"Reilly, you're losing it," he muttered as he drove toward the fire station, his hands trembling. "The whole goddamn town is losing it."

And deep down, he knew it wasn't just the mist.

It was whatever was in it.

Chapter Three

Isolation

By night's fall, Ash Hollow was no longer the sleepy small town it had been that morning. The mist was everywhere, choking every street and building, seeping into every crack like it had a personal vendetta against the town. The familiar hum of life—the barking dogs, the chatter of kids riding bikes, the buzz of Bert's Diner—was gone and replaced by silence. No, not silence. Something worse. The faint whispers. The distant scraping sounds. And the occasional scream, sharp and sudden, then cut short.

Sheriff Hank Reilly parked his cruiser in front of the fire station, the headlights cutting through the mist like a knife through blood. He turned off the engine and sat there momentarily, gripping the wheel so hard his knuckles went white. His uniform was torn, his arm still throbbing from where Tom Heller had clocked him earlier, and he was sure he'd blown his eardrum during his last shootout.

"Get it together, Hank," he muttered, staring into the mist. His reflection in the windshield looked pale, ghostly. "You're the sheriff. You don't have the luxury of losing your shit."

He opened the door, the thick red haze immediately curling into the car like it had been waiting for him. The metallic stench hit him again, that sharp tang of blood and rust, and he gagged, yanking his scarf up over his nose. His boots crunched on the gravel as he stepped out, his flashlight cutting wide, nervous arcs through the darkness.

"Clara," he called, his voice hoarse. "You in there?"

The heavy steel door of the fire station creaked open, and Clara Reed, his deputy, poked her head out. Her dark hair was tied back in a haphazard bun, and her face was pale with exhaustion. She held a shotgun in one hand and a flashlight in the other.

"Jesus, Sheriff," she muttered, stepping aside to let him in. "Took you long enough. Thought the mist got you."

"Almost did," Hank muttered as he stepped inside. The door slammed shut behind him with a metallic thud. "You are holding down the fort?"

"Barely," Clara said, gesturing to the room behind her. The station's garage had been converted into a makeshift shelter. About a dozen people were scattered across the space, huddled in small groups. Rick and his teenage son Billy sat near the firetruck, their backs against the tire, while Mary Trumbull—the town's kindergarten teacher—clutched her Bible in one hand and a damp rag in the other, pressing it to her nose like it was the only thing keeping her sane.

"Whole town's falling apart out there," Hank said, pulling up a chair and sinking into it with a groan. "People are hearing shit, seeing shit. Half of 'em have lost their goddamn minds."

"And the other half?" Clara asked.

"Dead," Hank said flatly, reaching into his jacket for a flask. He took a long swig before passing it to Clara. "Or hiding if they're smart."

She took the flask without a word, tilting it back and wincing as the cheap whiskey burned its way down. "This mist... it's doing something to people. Getting in their heads. Fucking with them."

"Tell me about it," Hank muttered, rubbing his temples. "I had to shoot Tom Heller this morning. The guy came at me with a wrench, grinning like he'd just won the lottery. He wasn't... there. Not really."

Clara nodded grimly. "The same thing happened with Sadie McCall. She stabbed Eric, the plumber at the diner, and started laughing like a joke. We had to knock her out cold." She gestured to the far corner of the room, where Sadie lay tied up with duct tape and rope. Her eyes were closed, but her chest rose and fell in shallow, uneven breaths.

"Any idea what we're dealing with?" Hank asked.

Clara let out a bitter laugh. "Yeah, Sheriff. I've got a fucking PhD in red death mist. I'll have it figured out by sunrise."

Hank smirked despite himself. "Fair point."

The hours crawled like molasses, each minute dragging slower than the last. Outside, the mist pressed against the station's windows, faintly glowing in the dim light of the emergency lanterns they'd managed to scrounge up. Every so often, one of the survivors would shift nervously, their eyes darting toward the windows as though they expected the mist to come crashing in any second.

"You hear that?" Rick whispered from his spot near the firetruck.

Clara turned her head sharply. "Hear what?"

Rick gestured toward the door. "There's... something out there."

Hank grabbed his revolver and stood, motioning for Clara to follow him. Together, they crept toward the door, their footsteps muffled by the thick tension in the air. Hank pressed his ear to the steel, holding a hand for silence.

At first, there was nothing. Just the faint hum of the mist, like the static of a dead radio station. But then he heard a soft, rhythmic scraping sound, like nails dragging across the metal.

"Fuck me," Clara muttered, raising her shotgun. "What is that?"

The sound grew louder, more deliberate. It circled the station, moving from one wall to the next as if testing for a weak spot. Then came the whispers. Low and guttural, spoken in a language neither of them recognized. It wasn't human.

"Shit," Hank muttered, his grip tightening on his revolver. "They're trying to get in."

Clara's voice dropped to a whisper. "Who the fuck are they?"

Hank didn't answer. He didn't have one.

They spent the next hour reinforcing the doors and windows with anything they could find—chains, metal beams, even an old ladder they'd propped against the back door. Rick and Billy helped, though the boy's hands shook so badly he nearly dropped his end of the ladder twice. Mary paced the room, muttering prayers under her breath.

"You think it's going to hold?" Clara asked, wiping sweat from her brow.

"It better," Hank said, his voice grim. "Because if it doesn't..."

A loud bang cut him off. Everyone froze. The sound came again, this time from the roof—a heavy, deliberate thud that sent dust raining down from the ceiling.

"They're on the roof," Rick whispered, his face pale.

"Stay calm," Hank barked, though his heart was pounding in his chest. He motioned for Clara to follow him, gesturing toward the ladder that led to the roof access hatch. "We need to see what we're dealing with."

Clara stared at him like he'd just suggested they vacation in hell. "Are you out of your fucking mind? You want to open the hatch?"

"Got a better idea?" Hank shot back. She didn't.

The climb up the ladder felt like an eternity. Hank pushed the hatch open an inch, peering through the gap. At first, he saw nothing but the swirling red mist. Then, a shape moved—tall and spindly, with limbs too long and a head tilted at an unnatural angle.

Hank's breath caught in his throat. The thing crouched low, its glowing eyes fixed on the hatch. And then it smiled.

"Shut the hatch," Clara hissed.

Hank slammed it shut, his hands shaking. "They're watching us," he said, his voice hollow. "They know we're in here."

"What the fuck do we do now?" Clara whispered.

Hank didn't answer. Because for the first time in his life, he didn't have a fucking clue.

Chapter Four

Revalations

Inside the fire station, the survivors sat in tense silence, the air so thick with fear it was hard to breathe. The red mist outside pressed against the windows like a living thing, faintly pulsing, almost like it had a heartbeat. Every so often, there would be noise—scratching, banging, or something faintly like laughter—and the entire group would freeze, hearts hammering, waiting for whatever came next.

Sheriff Hank Reilly sat at a metal table, staring at a crude map of Ash Hollow they'd drawn on a piece of cardboard. It was marked with circles and X's, each standing for something terrible: where they'd found bodies, where people had gone missing, where someone had "turned." He dragged a hand down his face, the stubble on his chin scratching his palm.

"You know," Hank muttered, his voice low, "I always thought if this town went to shit, it'd be because Bert finally poisoned everyone with that goddamn chili he makes for the festival."

Clara snorted, though it lacked any real humor. She was leaning against the wall, shotgun resting on her shoulder. "Hell, maybe it was the chili. Could explain the hallucinations."

Sitting cross-legged on the floor nearby, Rick let out a sharp laugh that quickly turned into a groan. His leg was still bleeding, the makeshift bandage doing little to stop it. "If we're going to die, I'd take chili over whatever the fuck's out there."

Hank glanced at the group. Most survivors were slumped in corners or huddled together, too drained to talk. Mary Trumbull sat on a bench, clutching her Bible and mumbling prayers under her breath, while Rachel, the teenager, stared blankly at the floor, her hands twitching every few seconds. Sadie McCall was still tied up in the corner, her lips moving silently, her eyes locked on the ceiling like she was conversing with something no one else could see.

"Sheriff," Clara said quietly, breaking the silence. "We can't stay here. You know that, right?"

Hank didn't answer right away. He just kept staring at the map, his jaw clenched. "Yeah," he said finally. "I know."

A loud thud from the roof made everyone jump. Hank shot to his feet, hand on his revolver. Clara aimed her shotgun at the ceiling, her heart pounding.

"Jesus Christ," Rick muttered, dragging himself back against the wall. "They're still out there."

"No shit, Rick," Clara snapped, her knuckles white as she gripped her gun.

The sound came again—another heavy thud, followed by a scraping noise that seemed to move across the roof. It wasn't random. It was deliberate, like something—or someone—was pacing.

"They're fucking with us," Hank muttered, more to himself than anyone else. "Testing us. Seeing how scared we are."

"Well, it's working," Rick said bitterly.

Hank grabbed his flashlight and motioned for Clara to follow him. "Come on. We need to see what's up there."

"Are you fucking serious?" Clara hissed, though she followed him anyway. "What are we going to do if it's one of them? Ask it nicely to piss off?"

Hank glanced back at her, a grim smile tugging at his lips. "We've got guns, flashlights, and a healthy amount of piss and vinegar. What else do we need?"

"Sanity," Clara muttered, though she tightened her grip on the shotgun.

They climbed the ladder slowly, their breathing loud in the quiet. Hank pushed the roof hatch open a crack and peeked out. The thick and suffocating mist swirled around the rooftop, but he could still see faint shapes moving in the haze.

"See anything?" Clara whispered.

Hank paused, his blood turning to ice. A figure stood at the roof's edge, its silhouette long and gaunt, like a scarecrow come to life. Its limbs were too thin, its head tilted at an impossible angle, and its glowing eyes pierced through the mist like twin embers.

"Yeah," Hank whispered back. "Something's up here."

The figure flicked, taking a step forward, its movements jerky and unnatural. It made no sound, but the mist around it seemed to ripple, reacting to its presence. Then it stopped and turned its head, staring directly at Hank.

"Fuck me," he muttered, ducking back down and slamming the hatch shut.

"What?" Clara demanded, her voice sharp. "What did you see?"

"Something... not human," Hank said, his voice tight. "It looked at me like it knew me. Like it was sizing me up."

"Oh, that's fucking great," Clara said, her voice dripping with sarcasm. "Add that to the list of things that'll haunt my dreams—assuming we live long enough to sleep."

They returned to the main room, where the survivors huddled in tense silence. Hank explained what he'd seen, though he kept his voice low, not wanting to send anyone into a full-blown panic. Not that it helped. Mary started crying softly, her prayers turning into incoherent muttering, and Rick began pacing—or limping—back and forth, muttering curses under his breath.

"This place isn't safe," Clara said, her voice firm. "You said it yourself, Sheriff. They're testing us. Eventually, they will stop testing and start tearing this place apart."

"Where the fuck are we supposed to go?" Rick snapped. "Outside? Into that?" He gestured to the windows, where the red mist glowed faintly, almost mockingly.

Hank sighed, rubbing a hand over his face. "The church," he said after a long moment. "It's got thicker walls, fewer windows. We can barricade it better than this place."

Clara raised an eyebrow. "The church? You think a fucking cross and some stained glass are going to save us from whatever the hell's out there?"

"It's not about the cross, Clara," Hank snapped. "It's about having a plan and following it. Do you have a better idea?"

Clara opened her mouth, then closed it again, clearly at a loss.

"That's what I thought," Hank said. He turned to the group. "We move at dawn. Everyone gets a flashlight, a weapon, whatever you can carry. We stay together, and we don't stop for anything. Got it?"

No one argued. No one even spoke. They all just nodded, their faces pale and grim.

The whispers started again around midnight. Soft at first, barely audible, but they grew louder, more insistent, filling the air like a dozen voices overlapping. They called out names, begged for help, and promised safety. And then they laughed—a low, guttural sound that sent chills down everyone's spines.

"They're fucking with us again," Clara muttered, her grip tightening on the shotgun. "I hate this goddamn town."

Hank didn't respond. He just stared out the window, his jaw clenched. The mist pulsed faintly, and for a moment, he thought he saw something move—something tall and thin, watching from the edge of the fog.

"We'll make it," he said softly, though he wasn't sure who he was trying to convince. The survivors, Clara, or himself.

Chapter Five

The Resistance

Dawn crept into Ash Hollow like a coward—weak, pale, and utterly useless. The red mist swallowed it, muting the sun's light and leaving the town bathed in an unnatural glow. Inside the fire station, no one moved. No one spoke. The survivors sat in tense silence, their nerves frayed and their hope dangling by a thread. The whispers outside had stopped again, but no one believed for a second that the mist was done with them.

Sheriff Hank Reilly stood by the garage door, shotgun slung over his shoulder and flashlight in hand. His eyes were bloodshot; his jaw clenched tight enough to crack a tooth. Clara Reed stood beside him, reloading her revolver slowly and deliberately. She looked like hell, but at least she was standing.

"You ready?" Hank asked, his voice rough.

Clara snorted. "Ready to walk into a sea of nightmare fog and probably get eaten by whatever the fuck's out there? Sure. Let's do this."

Hank smirked. "That's the spirit."

Behind them, the survivors were gearing up with whatever makeshift weapons they could find. Rick had a crowbar, and his son Billy clutched a flashlight like it was the only thing tethering him to reality. Mary Trumbull had finally stopped muttering prayers and gripped a fire axe with trembling hands. Even Sadie McCall, still tied up in the corner, had gone eerily quiet, her eyes flicking between the survivors and the door like she was waiting for something.

"Okay," Hank said, addressing the group. "We're heading to St. Luke's. It's got thicker walls, fewer windows, and—God help us—a basement. It's our best shot. Stay together, keep your lights on, and if you see or hear anything..." He paused, his gaze sweeping over the terrified faces. "Don't fucking stop."

Rick raised a hand, his voice trembling. "And if someone... you know... starts acting weird?"

Hank's jaw tightened. "You know what to do."

The room went silent.

The garage door opened slowly, the mechanical whine echoing in the oppressive quiet. The red mist poured in at once, curling around their ankles like it was alive. Hank stepped out first, shotgun at the ready, his flashlight cutting a narrow path through the haze. Clara followed, then Rick, Billy, Mary, and the rest of the group, their steps hesitant and their breaths shallow.

The mist was thicker than ever, and the metallic tang made breathing hard. It clung to their skin and clothes, entering their lungs. The silence was absolute, broken only by the crunch of gravel underfoot and the faint hum of the mist itself, like a low-frequency vibration that burrowed into their skulls.

"Jesus," Clara muttered, her eyes darting around the fog. "This shit's worse than Bert's chili cook-off."

Hank couldn't help but chuckle. "Keep talking like that. Maybe it'll scare 'em off."

They made their way down Main Street, the outlines of familiar buildings barely visible through the haze. The diner was a dark, hulking shape in the distance, its broken windows like black eyes staring out into the mist. The grocery store was even worse—its doors hung open, and something wet and dark stained the pavement out front. No one wanted to look too closely.

"Do you hear that?" Billy whispered, his voice barely audible.

"Hear what?" Rick asked, his grip tightening on the crowbar.

Billy shook his head, his eyes wide. "I... I thought I heard someone calling my name."

"Don't listen to it," Hank said sharply, his voice cutting through the tension. "It's the mist. It's trying to fuck with you."

"But it sounded like Mom," Billy said, his voice breaking. "She was—"

"It's not her!" Rick snapped, grabbing Billy by the arm. "Your mother's gone, Billy. That thing out there? It's not her."

Billy looked like he might argue, but looking at his father's face shut him up. He nodded, clutching his flashlight tighter.

"Keep moving," Hank said, his eyes scanning the mist. "We're almost there."

St. Luke's Church loomed ahead; its steeple was barely visible through the fog. The building was old, solid brick, with heavy wooden doors that looked like they could withstand a battering ram. As they approached, Hank felt a flicker of hope, but it was short-lived. The mist seemed to grow thicker around the church, the red glow pulsing faintly as though it didn't want them to reach it.

"Move faster," Clara hissed, her grip tightening on her revolver.

They made it to the front steps without incident, but when Hank grabbed the door handle, a sound erupted behind them—a low, guttural growl that sent a jolt of terror through the group.

"Shit!" Hank barked. "Inside! Now!"

The group scrambled up the steps as shapes appeared from the mist—tall, gaunt figures with glowing eyes and twisted limbs. Their movements were jerky, almost insect-like, as they crawled and stumbled toward the church. The air filled with whispers, louder now, overlapping and chaotic.

"Get the door open!" Clara shouted, firing her revolver at one of the creatures. The bullet hit its mark, but the thing didn't fall. It just staggered, tilting its head as though confused, before advancing.

Hank shoved the door open, waving the others inside. "Move your asses! Go, go, go!"

Rick and Billy were the first through, followed by Mary and the rest. Clara fired another shot before sprinting up the steps, slamming the door behind her just as one of the creatures lunged forward, its clawed hand scraping against the wood.

"Fuck!" she gasped, leaning against the door, her chest heaving. "What the hell are those things?"

"Nothing good," Hank said, bolting the door with a heavy wooden beam. He turned to the group, his eyes hard. "Everyone okay?"

No one answered. They were too busy catching their breath, their faces pale and drawn.

The whispers outside didn't stop. They grew louder and more insistent, pressing against the church walls like a physical force. The creatures scratched at the doors and windows, their glowing eyes visible through the cracks in the boarded-up glass.

"This isn't going to hold," Clara said, her voice tight. "You saw how strong those things are. They'll rip this place apart."

"We'll figure something out," Hank said, though he sounded unconvinced.

"And what if we can't?" Rick asked, his voice trembling. "What if this is it? What if—"

"Shut up!" Hank snapped, his voice echoing through the church. "We're not giving up. Not yet."

The room fell silent, save for the whispers outside.

Hank took a deep breath, his eyes scanning the frightened faces of the survivors. "This isn't over," he said quietly. "Not by a long shot."

And deep in the mist, the creatures kept waiting. Watching.

Chapter Six

Aftermath

The survivors sat huddled in the darkened church, the oppressive weight of the mist pressing against the walls like a suffocating vice. The heavy wooden doors rattled occasionally, accompanied by faint scratching noises and whispers that didn't sound quite human. The only light came from the flickering emergency lanterns they'd scavenged from the fire station, casting long, jittery shadows across the cracked walls of St. Luke's. No one spoke. No one dared.

Sheriff Hank Reilly leaned against the altar, his shotgun resting against his leg and his eyes fixed on the door. He hadn't blinked in minutes, the tension in his body so tight it felt like it might snap him in half. Clara Reed, his deputy, sat on the first pew, reloading her revolver with methodical precision. She looked calm, but Hank could see the faint tremor in her hands.

"You going to stare at that door all night?" Clara muttered, her voice low. "It's locked. Bolted. Holy-fucking-safety. Nothing's getting in."

"Yet," Hank said, not looking away. "Nothing's getting in yet."

Clara let out a dry laugh. "Optimistic as ever, Sheriff. Inspirational."

Hank finally tore his eyes away from the door to glance at her. "You want optimism? Wrong guy. Bert's Diner used to have one of those inspirational quote calendars. Maybe that survived the apocalypse."

"Oh yeah?" Clara smirked, though it didn't reach her eyes. "What's today's quote? 'Hang in there, you're only completely fucked for the foreseeable future'?"

Hank almost laughed, but it came out more like a dry cough. "Something like that."

The whispers started again, louder this time, crawling through the cracks in the boarded-up windows. They weren't in English. Hell, they weren't in any language Hank had ever heard, but somehow, the meaning came through clear as day: Let us in. We're waiting.

Rick, pacing near the back of the sanctuary, froze. "Did you hear that?" he whispered, his voice trembling. "They're... they're talking now."

"We've been hearing that shit for hours," Clara said, not bothering to look at him. "Congratulations, you've caught up."

"No," Rick snapped, his voice rising. "It's different now. They're... They're calling my name."

Hank stood, his shotgun in hand. "Rick," he said, his tone low and calm. "It's not real. You know that. The mist is fucking with your head."

Rick turned to face him, his eyes wide and panicked. "But what if it's not? What if—what if someone's out there? What if it's Billy's mom? She—"

"She's dead, Rick," Hank cut him off, his voice harsh. "You know that. You saw it."

Rick flinched like he'd been slapped. Sitting in the corner with his flashlight clutched, Billy looked up at the sound of his name. His face was pale, and his eyes were hollow like he was barely holding it together.

"Dad?" Billy said softly. "You're scaring me."

Rick's shoulders sagged, and he sat down hard on the nearest pew, burying his face in his hands. "I'm sorry," he muttered. "I just... I don't know how much more of this I can take."

Hank sighed and stepped closer, his voice softening. "None of us do, Rick. But losing it now isn't going to help anyone. We've made it this far. We must keep going."

Rick let out a bitter laugh. "Keep going where? We're trapped in a goddamn church surrounded by demon fog. What's the plan, Sheriff? Wait until it eats us alive?"

Hank didn't answer. He didn't have an answer.

The scratching at the doors grew louder and more insistent as if whatever was outside was tired of waiting. The survivors froze, their breaths hitching, as a low, guttural growl echoed through the sanctuary. It wasn't human. It wasn't even close.

"Oh, fuck this," Clara muttered, standing and aiming her shotgun at the door. "If they want to come in, let's give 'em a fucking welcome party."

"Hold your fire," Hank said, stepping between her and the door. "You won't scare them off; you'll just waste ammo."

"Waste ammo?" Clara barked, her voice rising. "You think we'll live long enough to run out of it?"

Before Hank could respond, Sadie McCall, the woman they'd tied up earlier, let out a sharp laugh from her corner of the sanctuary. It was a horrible sound—high-pitched and broken like it had been dragged out of her against her will.

"Sadie," Hank said, his voice tense. "You okay over there?"

She lifted her head to look at him, and the sight sent a chill down his spine. Her eyes were black—completely black, like the mist had crawled inside her and hollowed her out. She grinned, her lips pulling back too far, exposing bloody gums and teeth that didn't look quite right.

"They're not outside anymore," she whispered, her voice guttural and distorted. "They're already here."

The scratching stopped.

The lanterns flickered, dimming light until the sanctuary was bathed in shadows. The temperature dropped sharply, and the air grew thick as the mist had finally seeped inside. Hank's grip tightened on his shotgun as he scanned the room, his pulse hammering in his ears.

"Everybody stay calm," he said, though his voice wavered. "Lights up. Check the corners."

Rick fumbled with his flashlight, nearly dropping it as he swung the beam toward the back of the room. For a moment, there was nothing—just empty pews and flickering shadows. But then a shape moved—a tall, spindly figure with too-long limbs and glowing eyes that burned like coals.

"Jesus Christ!" Rick shouted, stumbling back.

The thing stepped forward, its movements jerky and unnatural, like a puppet with its strings tangled. It tilted its head, staring at the group with an unblinking gaze that seemed to bore straight into their souls.

"Light it up!" Clara yelled, firing her shotgun.

The blast hit the creature square in the chest but didn't fall. It staggered, the mist around it rippling like water, but then it straightened and let out a sound—a high-pitched, chittering laugh that made Hank's skin crawl.

"Fuck me," Hank muttered, raising his shotgun. "Everybody, keep your lights on it. Don't let it move."

The survivors scrambled, their flashlight beams converging on the creature. It hissed, the glow in its eyes flickered, and it seemed to falter momentarily.

"It doesn't like the light," Clara said, reloading her gun. "Keep it pinned."

"Pinned for what?" Rick shouted. "You think it's just going to fucking give up?"

The creature lunged, moving faster than anything that size had any right to. Hank fired, the shotgun blast echoing through the sanctuary, and the thing let out a horrible screech as it collapsed into the mist. The red fog swirled around it, pulling it back into the shadows, and then it was gone.

But the whispers didn't stop.

"That's it," Clara said, her voice shaking as she lowered her gun. "We're fucked. They're inside. They're already inside."

Hank turned to the group, his face grim. "We're not done yet."

Clara let out a bitter laugh. "Not done? Sheriff, we're in the middle of a Stephen King novel, and you're telling me we're not done? What the fuck is the plan, huh? Enlighten me."

Hank met her gaze, his jaw tightening. "The plan is we survive. Whatever it takes."

"Whatever it takes," Clara echoed, shaking her head. "You think that's enough?"

Hank didn't answer. He reloaded his shotgun, the sound echoing through the sanctuary like a promise.

The mist wasn't done with them. And neither was he.

Chapter Seven

The Descent

The mist seemed angrier now, its crimson glow pulsing brighter and faster, like a beating heart on the verge of exploding. The whispers had returned, louder and more deliberate, speaking in overlapping tones that wormed their way into the survivors' ears. No one could make out the words—if they were words—but the intent was clear: submission, despair, death.

Inside the church, Sheriff Hank Reilly paced near the altar, shotgun in one hand, flashlight in the other. The survivors were scattered in small groups, each looking more hollowed out than the last. The toll of the previous twenty-four hours—hell, the previous two hours—had pushed most of them to their breaking points. And Hank didn't know how much more any of them could take.

He sure as shit didn't know how much more he could take.

"Alright," Hank said, stopping in front of the group. "We've got two options: we can sit here and wait for whatever's out there to come in and rip us apart, or we can do something about it."

"Do what?" Rick snapped, still holding his crowbar like it was his lifeline. "What the fuck are we supposed to do, Hank? Walk out there and ask the mist nicely to leave us alone?"

"Not exactly," Hank said, his tone clipped. "We don't know what this thing is or what it wants, but we know one thing: it doesn't like the light. We use that. We hit it back."

"Hit it back?" Clara raised an eyebrow, leaning against the wall with her shotgun slung over her shoulder. "Hank, I hate to be the one to piss on your parade, but this isn't a fucking bar fight. These things... whatever they are... they're not scared of us."

"No, but they're scared of the light," Hank said, his eyes darting to the lanterns they'd scattered around the church. "We've got lanterns, flashlights, a generator in the basement. We can rig something. Make this place a goddamn spotlight."

"And then what?" Mary Trumbull whispered, clutching her Bible so tightly her knuckles were white. "What happens when the lights don't work? What happens when they just... keep coming?"

"Then we fight," Hank said. "Or we die."

"Fantastic pep talk," Clara muttered under her breath. "I'm fucking inspired."

The survivors moved quickly, gathering supplies from the church and its basement—lanterns, extension cords, tools—anything that could hold or generate light. Clara found an old floodlight tucked away in a storage closet, and Rick nearly cried when he unearthed a roll of duct tape.

"You could fix the goddamn apocalypse with this," he muttered, holding the tape like it was a holy relic.

"Yeah, well, don't get too attached," Clara tossed him a flashlight. "We're still fucked either way."

Despite the grim situation, the work gave everyone a slight sense of purpose. Even Mary had stopped muttering prayers long enough to help Clara secure the floodlight to the altar, though her hands trembled the entire time.

"Where's Rachel?" Billy asked suddenly, his voice breaking the tense silence.

Hank froze. He turned, scanning the sanctuary, but the teenager was nowhere to be seen. "Shit," he muttered, gripping his shotgun. "Anyone see where she went?"

No one answered.

"Goddammit," Clara snapped. "How the fuck do we lose someone in a church?"

The whispers grew louder as if in response, and Hank felt a cold knot of dread twist in his gut. "Stay here," he said, his voice low. "I'll find her."

"I'm coming with you," Clara said at once, cocking her shotgun.

"No," Hank said firmly. "Stay here. If something happens to me, you're the only one who can handle that generator."

Clara opened her mouth to argue, but the look on Hank's face stopped her. "Fine," she said, her tone clipped. "But if you're not back in ten minutes, I'm coming after your dumb ass."

"Deal," Hank said, and with that, he disappeared into the shadows.

The back hall of the church was eerily quiet. The whispers were muted but still present like they were hiding just beyond the edge of hearing. Hank's flashlight cut through the darkness, the beam shaking slightly as his hand trembled.

"Rachel," he called softly. "You out here? Come on, kid, this isn't funny."

No answer.

Hank swallowed hard, his throat dry. The air felt heavier here, colder, and every step he took echoed like a gunshot. He passed a series of old wooden doors, each leading to storage rooms or small offices, and gripped his shotgun tighter.

"Rachel," he said again, louder this time. "If you're out here, say something."

A faint laugh echoed through the hall, high-pitched and broken. Hank froze.

"Rachel?" he called, his voice tense.

The laugh came again, this time from behind one of the doors. Hank turned, his flashlight illuminating the cracked wood. His heart hammered in his chest as he reached for the doorknob, every instinct screaming at him to turn around and run.

Instead, he kicked the door open.

The room was empty, save for the faint outline of Rachel in the far corner. She was sitting on the floor, her knees pulled to her chest, her face buried in her arms. Her flashlight lay next to her, the beam flickering weakly.

"Rachel," Hank said softly, stepping into the room. "It's okay. I've got you."

She didn't move.

Hank took another step closer, lowering his shotgun slightly. "Come on, kid. Let's get back to the others."

Rachel lifted her head slowly, and Hank felt his stomach drop. Her eyes were black—utterly black like the mist had crawled inside her and eaten her from the inside out. She smiled, her lips stretching too far, and whispered, "They're here."

The door slammed shut behind him.

Back in the sanctuary, the survivors heard the crash and the muffled sound of Hank's voice shouting something incoherent. Clara bolted upright, her shotgun at the ready.

"Stay here," she barked, but Rick grabbed her arm.

"What if it's already too late?" he asked, his voice shaking.

"Then I guess we're all fucked," Clara said, pulling free. "But I'm not sitting here waiting to die."

She disappeared into the hallway, her flashlight bobbing wildly as she ran.

When Clara found Hank, he was crouched against the room's far wall, his shotgun aimed at Rachel. She was standing now, her head tilted at an unnatural angle, her black eyes fixed on him.

"Don't," Hank said, his voice shaking. "Don't come any closer."

Rachel took a step forward, her movements jerky and unnatural, like a puppet with its strings tangled. The mist seemed to swirl around her feet, seeping into the room like it was alive.

"Rachel," Clara said, her voice low. "You in there, kid?"

The girl didn't answer. Instead, she smiled wider, her teeth stained red, and said, "It's too late. You can't stop them."

"Bullshit," Clara said, raising her shotgun. "We've stopped plenty of things before. You're just another bump in the road."

Rachel laughed—a horrible, guttural sound that sent chills down Clara's spine. "You don't understand," she said. "This isn't a fight. It's a feeding."

Before Clara could respond, Rachel lunged.

The struggle was quick and brutal and left Hank and Clara panting on the floor, Rachel's body motionless between them. The whispers outside grew louder, almost deafening now, and the pulsing glow of the mist seeped through the cracks in the walls.

"We can't stay here," Clara said, her voice breathless. "This place isn't safe anymore."

"No shit," Hank muttered, wiping blood from his face. "We need to move. Now."

"Where?" Clara demanded. "There's nowhere left to go."

Hank stared at her for a long moment, his jaw tightening. "Then we make a stand," he said finally. "If this is the end, we go out swinging."

Clara let out a bitter laugh. "Great. Can't wait."

The two of them hauled Rachel's body into the hallway and returned to the sanctuary, where the survivors were waiting with wide, terrified eyes. The whispers were louder than ever, and the mist began to seep under the doors.

"Alright," Hank said, raising his shotgun. "Let's give these fuckers a fight they'll never forget."

And with that, the doors burst open.

Chapter Eight

The Last Stand

The doors of St. Luke's exploded inward, splintering into shards that flew across the sanctuary like shrapnel. The mist surged behind them, writhing and pulsing as it swallowed the flickering light from the lanterns. The survivors screamed, their terror echoing through the church as the glowing-eyed creatures followed the mist, their twisted forms stepping into the open. This was it—the end.

Sheriff Hank Reilly stood at the altar, his shotgun raised, the remaining survivors huddled around him. The floodlights flickered wildly, and the generator let out a strained whine as if it, too, knew this fight was unwinnable.

"Fuck this day," Hank muttered under his breath, gripping his shotgun so tightly his knuckles turned white. He fired into the mist, the shot echoing through the sanctuary, but the creature he hit barely flinched. It staggered, shook itself off, and kept coming.

"Fall back!" Hank shouted. "Get to the altar—stay in the light!"

Clara Reed grabbed Billy by the arm and dragged him toward the center of the sanctuary as the mist grew closer. Rick was gone. Mary was gone. Hell, half the town was gone. And there wasn't a goddamn thing anyone could do about it.

"Clara!" Hank barked, pointing toward the generator. "Keep the lights running!"

She glanced at him, her face pale but determined. "You want me to babysit a dying generator while mist monsters eat us alive? Fantastic fucking plan, Sheriff!"

"Just do it!" Hank roared, firing another shot as one of the creatures lunged toward the group. The blast hit it square in the chest, sending it sprawling back into the fog. But Hank knew it wouldn't stay down. None of them did.

Clara sprinted to the generator, yanking the ripcord like her life depended on it. The floodlights surged, cutting through the mist and forcing the creatures back. For a moment, it felt like they might have a chance.

And then the generator sputtered and died.

The sanctuary plunged into near-total darkness. The mist surged forward, thicker and more oppressive than ever, and the creatures moved with it. Their glowing eyes flickered like dying coals as they closed in on the survivors.

Billy screamed as one of the creatures lunged for him, its claws outstretched. Hank stepped in front of the boy, swinging the butt of his shotgun into the creature's face. It staggered, hissing, but another one was already behind it, its skeletal fingers reaching for Hank's throat.

"Goddammit!" Clara screamed, firing her revolver wildly into the mist. "There's too many!"

Hank knew she was right. He also knew they didn't have a choice. If the creatures were going to take them, they would make it a fight.

"Get behind me!" Hank shouted, dragging Billy closer to the altar. His gaze flicked to the glowing cross above the altar. Its faint white light was the only thing the mist hadn't consumed. And then it hit him.

"Clara!" he shouted. "The cross—they don't like the cross! Get it down!"

Clara glanced up at the glowing symbol, her eyes narrowing. "You've got to be kidding me."

"Just fucking do it!" Hank yelled, firing his last shotgun shell into the mist. One of the creatures shrieked and dissolved, but two more took its place.

Clara didn't argue. She climbed onto the altar, her boots slipping on the blood-streaked floor, and reached for the cross. It was bolted to the wall, its metal frame rusted with age.

"It's stuck!" she shouted.

"Then pull harder!" Hank yelled back, swinging the shotgun like a club as another creature lunged at him.

Clara gritted her teeth and yanked on the cross with everything she had. It came free with a loud crack, the glowing metal nearly slipping from her hands. The moment it was free, the mist recoiled violently, the creatures screaming in unison as the light from the cross burned brighter.

"It's working!" Billy shouted, his voice breaking with hope. "They're scared of it!"

"Good!" Hank barked, grabbing Clara's arm. "Then let's finish this."

With Clara holding the cross high above her head, the survivors pushed forward, forcing the creatures back. The mist writhed and twisted but couldn't get close to the light. The creatures hissed and screamed, their forms flickering like dying flames.

"Keep moving!" Hank shouted. "Don't stop!"

The mist seemed to sense it was losing. The whispers grew louder and more frantic, begging and threatening in equal measure: "Let us in. Let us take you. You belong to us."

"Go fuck yourself," Clara muttered under her breath, gripping the cross tighter.

They reached the church's front doors, the mist pressing against them like a physical wall. Hank motioned for Billy to open the doors; his flashlight focused on the creatures lingering at the light's edges.

"Are we going out there?" Billy asked, his voice trembling.

"We're not staying here," Hank said. "Now open the damn doors."

Billy nodded and threw the doors open. The mist outside was thicker than ever, but the light from the cross seemed to cut through it, creating a narrow path that led toward the hills outside of town.

"Go!" Hank barked, shoving Billy forward.

The group ran, the light from the cross their only shield against the encroaching fog. The whispers followed them, growing louder and angrier with every step, but the creatures couldn't get close. The cross burned too brightly, its glow cutting through the darkness like a beacon.

By the time they reached the edge of the mist, the survivors were gasping for air, their bodies battered and broken. The light from the cross had begun to dim, flickering like an old lightbulb on its last legs.

"Is this it?" Clara panted, glancing at Hank. "Is this as far as we go?"

Hank didn't answer. He just kept walking, his eyes fixed on the faint outline of the hills ahead. The mist began to thin, its glow fading as they moved farther from the town. The whispers grew softer, then stopped altogether.

And then, just like that, the mist was gone.

The survivors collapsed on the grass outside town, the early morning sun finally breaking through the clouds. For the first time in what felt like an eternity, the air was clear, free of the metallic tang that had clung to their lungs. Hank dropped to his knees, the cross clattering beside him.

"Is it over?" Billy asked, his voice small.

Hank looked back at the town, now barely visible through the trees. The mist was gone, and so were the creatures. The silence felt like a blessing.

"Yeah," Hank said finally, his voice hoarse. "It's over."

Clara let out a shaky laugh, wiping sweat and blood from her face. "If I never see another cloud of fog in my life, it'll be too soon."

The survivors sat silently, the weight of what they'd been through settling over them. They didn't know what had caused the mist or why it had come. And maybe they never would. But they were alive. And that was enough.

For now.

Epilogue

The Quiet After

The air outside Ash Hollow was clean, sharp, and impossibly quiet. Hank Reilly sat on the hood of his cruiser, staring back toward the town he'd spent most of his life protecting. Or what was left of it? The rooftops of St. Luke's, Bert's Diner, and the water tower barely peeked above the trees in the distance. There is no red mist. No glowing-eyed horrors. Just silence.

But it didn't feel like peace. It felt like the pause before another storm.

"You think it's gone?" Clara Reed asked, leaning against the side of the cruiser. Her shotgun rested beside her, the barrel streaked with blood and ash. She looked worse for wear—scratches down her face, a patch of dried blood on her temple, and dark circles under her eyes—but she was still standing. That was more than they could say for most.

Hank shook his head. "Gone? Maybe. But over? Hell no." He took a swig from the dented flask he kept in his jacket and held it to Clara. She took it without hesitation, grimacing as the cheap whiskey burned its way down her throat.

"You think it'll come back?" Billy's voice broke the quiet. The kid was sitting on a tree stump a few feet away, clutching the flashlight that had survived the ordeal. He hadn't spoken much since they'd made it out. Hell, he hadn't cried either and just sat there, hollow-eyed, as if he hadn't entirely caught up to what had happened.

Hank sighed, running a hand over his stubble. "I don't know, kid. Maybe."

Billy looked at the ground, his grip tightening on the flashlight. "If it does..., what do we do?"

"We fight," Clara said flatly. "Same as we did before."

Hank glanced at her, raising an eyebrow. "You make it sound like that went well."

"Well, we're still breathing," Clara said, smirking faintly. "Call it a win."

Hank didn't laugh. Instead, he turned his gaze back to the horizon. The sun was setting now, casting long shadows over the hills. The warm orange glow was a welcome change from the relentless crimson they'd been trapped in for the last day. But even as the light faded, he couldn't shake the feeling that something was still waiting.

The survivors—what was left of them—had scattered. Billy sat quietly, lost in his thoughts. Despite her tough exterior, Clara looked like she might collapse any second. And Hank? Hank was trying to figure out what the hell to do next. He'd spent his whole life solving problems, fixing things, and keeping the peace. But this? This was something else. Something bigger.

"I keep thinking about what Sadie said," Clara said suddenly, breaking the silence.

Hank turned to her, frowning. "Sadie? You mean before she...?"

"Yeah." Clara leaned back against the cruiser, staring up at the sky. "She said, 'It's not a fight. It's a feeding.'" She glanced at Hank. "What the hell do you think she meant by that?"

Hank sighed, rubbing his temples. "I don't know. Maybe the mist... whatever it was... wasn't here to take over. Maybe it just wanted to break us. Make us scared. Make us... I don't know... easier to digest."

Clara let out a humorless laugh. "So what? We're just snacks for some cosmic fog monsters?"

"Something like that," Hank muttered.

"That's fucking fantastic." Clara shook her head, her smirk fading. "And we don't even know where it came from."

"Doesn't matter," Hank said. "Where it came from, why it's here—it's gone. That's what matters."

Clara looked at him, her expression stern. "But what if it's not?"

A cool breeze swept through the trees, rustling the leaves. It was the kind of sound Hank had taken for granted before the mist came. It felt eerie like the world was still holding its breath.

"Hey, Sheriff," Clara said after a long pause. "You ever think about leaving this town? You know, before all this?"

Hank chuckled dryly. "All the time. But you don't leave Ash Hollow. People come here; they get stuck. It's like this place has roots."

"Well, maybe it's time to cut those roots," Clara muttered, looking back toward the faint outline of the town. "There's not much left to save."

Hank didn't respond. He just stared into the distance, his hand resting on the butt of his shotgun. Maybe Clara was right. Maybe there wasn't anything left worth staying for. But leaving didn't feel right either. Not yet.

Billy finally stood, his flashlight still clutched tightly in his hands. "What do we do now?" he asked, his voice quiet but steady.

Hank didn't answer right away. He looked at Clara, then at the kid, then back at the fading horizon. "We stick together," he said finally. "And we keep moving."

"Moving where?" Clara asked, raising an eyebrow.

"Anywhere but here," Hank said, grabbing the cross they'd pulled from the church. Its faint glow had dimmed, but it was still there, flickering like the last ember of a dying fire. He held it up, letting its light cut through the growing darkness. "But if that thing comes back..."

He glanced over his shoulder at the ruins of Ash Hollow, the ghost town barely visible through the trees. His jaw tightened.

"...if it comes back, we'll be ready."

The three set off into the fading light, leaving the town behind. The whispers were gone. The mist was gone. But the scars? The scars weren't going anywhere.

And somewhere deep in the hills, where the trees grew thick, and the air grew cold, the earth shuddered—just slightly, quietly, as something beneath it had stirred.

Waiting. Watching.

Hungry.

Sealed Inside

Chapter One

Specimen X

The storm outside raged like a personal welcome from hell. Dr. Evelyn Harper yanked her coat tighter around her shoulders as the wind whipped rain sideways, soaking her pants before she even reached the lab's main entrance.

"Jesus Christ," she muttered, struggling with the keycard against the scanner. The damn thing always froze in harsh weather. She swiped it again, harder this time, as though that would help.

ACCESS GRANTED.

"About fucking time," Evelyn hissed under her breath, stomping into the lobby of the preservation lab, an ultramodern facility buried in the middle of nowhere. As the glass doors slid shut behind her, the roar of the storm was replaced by the sterile hum of fluorescent lights.

She shook herself off, water pooling at her feet, and glanced around. The place looked as lifeless as ever. Everything was white, chrome, or glass—minimalist and cold, like walking into a high-tech mausoleum.

"Welcome back, Dr. Harper," the receptionist bot chirped, its automated voice too chipper for Evelyn's current mood.

"Yeah, thanks, Hal," she said, tossing her soaked coat over one arm. She wasn't in the mood to pretend the damn thing was alive.

"Dr. Harper, you are late," a clipped voice called from down the hall. Evelyn turned to see Dr. Malcolm Hayes, the lab's director, standing there with his arms crossed. He always looked like he was auditioning for the role of "Overbearing Asshole" in some low-budget office drama.

Evelyn forced a smile. "And good evening to you too, Dr. Hayes. You look like shit as usual."

"Professional as ever," he said, rolling his eyes. "We're behind schedule. There's an issue with—"

"Oh, let me guess," she interrupted, holding a hand. "The cryo units are acting up again, the budget's blown, and you're blaming me because you can't figure out how to fix it?"

Malcolm scowled. "Just... get down to the stasis wing. Now."

Evelyn gave him a mock salute, biting back a grin as she walked past. "Aye, aye, Captain Buzzkill."

As Evelyn made her way through the labyrinth of corridors, the sense of unease that always came with this place crept up on her. It wasn't the pathogens—they were locked away behind multiple levels of security. No, it was the specimens.

Every time she passed one of the stasis chambers, she could feel their presence—dozens of extinct creatures frozen in time, suspended in a blue-tinted glow. Saber-toothed cats, dodos, even a mammoth calf. It was like walking through the world's creepiest zoo.

Then there was the one chamber they didn't talk about.

Specimen X.

It wasn't listed in the official records. Nobody knew what it was except for the higher-ups, and they weren't sharing. Evelyn had only caught glimpses of the containment protocols: pressure sensors, redundant locks, and an air filtration system that could probably survive a nuclear blast. Whatever was in there, it was serious.

She glanced at the chamber as she passed it, the hair on the back of her neck standing up. It looked no different from the others—just a frosted glass panel and a soft blue glow—but something about it always felt... off.

"Don't stare too long," a voice said behind her, startling her so badly she nearly screamed.

She spun around to find Jason, the lab tech, grinning at her like a kid who just got away with stealing candy.

"Jesus, Jason! Are you trying to give me a fucking heart attack?"

"Sorry," he said, not looking sorry at all. "You were just standing there, staring at it. I figured you needed a little reminder."

"Reminder of what? That you're an asshole?"

"Nope. It's a reminder that the last guy who stared at that chamber for too long quit the next day. He said he couldn't sleep anymore. Said he kept seeing... shapes."

Evelyn rolled her eyes, but her stomach tightened. Jason had a bad habit of turning everything into a ghost story. "Thanks for the bedtime story, Jason. Now, excuse me, I have actual work to do."

Jason raised his hands in mock surrender. "Sure thing, Dr. Harper. Just don't say I didn't warn you."

She walked away, shaking her head, but couldn't resist glancing back at the chamber one last time.

Evelyn found the cryo units in the stasis wing exactly how she expected them: flashing red warning lights and throwing a hissy fit like spoiled children. She groaned and pulled up the diagnostic interface.

"Okay, what the hell is it this time?" she muttered, scrolling through the error logs.

"Let me guess," she added in a mock robotic voice. "Critical systems failure. Don't hesitate to get in touch with your system administrator. Oh wait, that's me!"

She snorted at her joke, but it didn't make her feel better. The logs showed a cascade of minor failures all over the wing as if the entire system was slowly falling apart. Again.

As she rebooted the units, her mind drifted back to Specimen X.

"Shapes," she said aloud, mimicking Jason's dramatic tone. "What a load of—"

A sharp hiss interrupted her thoughts.

She froze. The sound was faint but unmistakable—the sound of pressure equalizing, like a seal breaking.

Her eyes darted to the glass chambers lining the room. They all looked intact.

But she couldn't shake the feeling that something was... watching her.

Chapter Two

A Glitch in the System

Evelyn sat in her office, leaning back in her chair and nursing a cup of stale coffee. She stared at the computer screen, trying to make sense of the endless streams of diagnostic data.

"This place is held together with duct tape and prayers," she muttered, blowing on the coffee as if it could fix her mood.

The sound of her office door creaking open startled her, and she nearly spilled the coffee down her lab coat. Jason poked his head in, grinning like a kid caught sneaking into a movie.

"Guess who didn't die in the stasis wing today?" he said, plopping himself in the chair opposite her.

"Me," Evelyn replied dryly. "Because I'm the one who does the work around here."

"Wow, someone's grumpy," Jason said, pulling a candy bar from his pocket and slowly unwrapping it obnoxiously. "Want some? Sugar's good for the soul."

"Unless you're diabetic, in which case it's just good for your funeral," she snapped, rubbing her temples.

Jason smirked. "I see you've been working on your people skills. Charming as ever."

Before Evelyn could retort, a low-pitched alarm began to hum through the facility. It wasn't loud—yet—but it was persistent and immediately set her teeth on edge.

"What the fuck now?" she muttered, pushing herself up from the chair. Jason followed her as she marched down the corridor toward the control room.

"Maybe it's just a drill?" he offered.

"Drills don't sound like that, Jason. That's the 'something is royally fucked' alarm."

In the control room, Dr. Malcolm Hayes was already pacing in front of the central console, his expression a mix of frustration and poorly masked panic.

"Harper!" he barked as she entered. "Where the hell have you been?"

"Fixing your mistakes, as usual," Evelyn said, brushing past him to get to the monitor. "What's going on?"

"We're getting pressure fluctuations in stasis chambers two through six," Malcolm said, his voice tight. "I can't get the system to stabilize."

Evelyn frowned and leaned over the console, tapping furiously at the keyboard. "Chambers two through six... that's the main wing. Wait. What about Specimen X?"

Malcolm shot her a look. "That's contained. Focus on the rest."

"That's contained," she mimicked under her breath. "Sure, it is."

Jason leaned over her shoulder, popping the rest of his candy bar into his mouth. "Hey, what if—"

"Shut up, Jason," she snapped, her eyes glued to the screen.

The pressure readings weren't just fluctuating—they were spiking, then crashing, like the system was having a full-blown meltdown. And then there it was: Specimen X's chamber flashing yellow on the screen. Not red—not yet—but enough to make her stomach twist.

"Malcolm," she said, her voice lower now, more serious. "We've got a problem."

"I thought I told you—"

"Shut up and look!" She pointed at the screen, her finger hovering over the warning symbol blinking next to Specimen X's containment unit.

Malcolm's face paled. "That's... that can't be right. The redundancies should prevent any—"

"Yeah, well, the redundancies are flipping us off right now," she interrupted. "Something's wrong with the seals. There's a pressure leak."

Jason snorted nervously. "Maybe it's just a glitch, you know? Like when my coffee machine says it's out of water, but it's not?"

Evelyn glared at him. "Yeah, Jason, sure. A glitch. Let's just hope the universe is as forgiving as your fucking Keurig."

The three of them scrambled to the stasis wing, Malcolm barking orders into his comm device while Evelyn tried not to lose her shit entirely. The alarm was louder here, a low, pulsing drone that made the hair on her arms stand on end.

Evelyn immediately noticed the condensation in Specimen X's chamber as they entered the wing. The frost that usually coated the glass was melting, tiny rivulets of water running down its surface.

"Holy shit," Jason whispered, his usual sarcasm replaced by genuine fear.

"Quiet," Malcolm snapped, though his voice was shaking.

Evelyn approached the chamber cautiously, eyes scanning the monitors built into the frame. The pressure inside was dropping steadily, and she could hear that faint hiss again—the sound of air escaping.

"Is it me," Jason said, his voice barely above a whisper, "or is it... breathing?"

Evelyn froze. She hadn't wanted to think about it, but now that he'd said it, she couldn't unhear it—the faint rise and fall of something massive inside the chamber.

"No," she said firmly. "It's not breathing. That's just... it's just condensation patterns messing with your head."

Jason raised an eyebrow. "Uh-huh. Tell that to the goosebumps crawling up my arms right now."

Evelyn turned to Malcolm. "We need to lock this wing down. Now."

"Lock it down?" he repeated, his voice sharp. "We don't even know what we're dealing with yet."

"Exactly. Which is why I'd rather not be standing here when it decides to introduce itself."

Malcolm hesitated, and Evelyn felt her frustration boil over. "Goddammit, Malcolm, do something useful for once in your life!"

With a growl, Malcolm stormed over to the control panel on the wall and began inputting commands. "Fine. But if this turns out to be nothing—"

"Yeah, yeah, you'll hold it over my head forever. Just do it!"

The room fell silent as they waited for the locks to engage. But instead of the reassuring click of containment seals, a new sound filled the air: a deep, resonant crack.

Evelyn turned slowly, her heart hammering in her chest. The glass on Specimen X's chamber was splintering, thin spider web fractures spreading outward from the center.

Jason took a step back, his face white as a sheet. "Oh, fuck this. Fuck. This."

"Agreed," Evelyn said, already backing toward the exit. "Time to go."

Chapter Three

The Awakening

The room was silent except for the sound of cracking glass. It wasn't loud—subtle, like the sound you'd hear if you pressed too hard on an ice cube—but it made Evelyn's heart feel like it was about to claw out of her chest.

"Holy shit," Jason whispered, his voice so quiet she barely heard him over the sound of her breathing. "It's going to break. The glass is fucking breaking."

"No shit, Sherlock," Evelyn snapped, not taking her eyes off the fractures spreading across the chamber. "What's your next brilliant observation? That we're about to fucking die?"

Jason didn't respond. For once, he didn't have a comeback. That might have scared her more than the glass cracking.

Standing frozen by the control panel, Malcolm finally snapped out of it and slammed a hand on the emergency lockdown button. A deep mechanical groan reverberated as metal shutters slid over the stasis chambers.

"Containment engaged," the computer announced in its robotic monotone. "Threat level: critical."

Evelyn glanced at the chamber, praying the shutters would come down fast enough. The cracks were spidering out faster now, spreading like veins.

But then it happened.

The glass gave way with an earsplitting shatter. Pressurized air and frost hit the room, stumbling backward Evelyn and Jason. The shutters froze mid-descent, leaving Specimen X's chamber fully exposed.

"Motherfucker," Evelyn hissed, pulling herself up from the floor. She stared into the chamber, her mind screaming to run, but her legs refused to move.

Specimen X was... alive.

It moved slowly at first, like waking up from the world's worst nap. Its body was massive, covered in something that looked like both scales and fur, and its limbs—Jesus Christ, its limbs—were too long, bending in ways that made Evelyn's stomach churn.

"What the fuck is that?" Jason's voice cracked as he scrambled to his feet.

"I don't know," Evelyn whispered, not trusting her voice to be any louder. "But it shouldn't be moving. It shouldn't be alive."

Specimen X's head turned slowly toward them, revealing a face that was both alien and disturbingly human. Its eyes—if you could call them that—were black and glossy, reflecting the room like polished obsidian.

It let out a low, guttural noise between a growl and a sigh. The sound vibrated through Evelyn's chest, making her ribs ache.

"Okay," Jason said, his voice high-pitched and panicked. "I vote we get the fuck out of here."

"For once," Evelyn muttered, "I agree with you."

Malcolm, however, wasn't moving. He stood frozen, staring at the creature like he couldn't decide whether to be terrified or fascinated.

"Malcolm," Evelyn said sharply, grabbing his arm. "Move your ass!"

"It's... it's beautiful," he murmured, his eyes wide.

"It's a fucking death sentence, is what it is!" she snapped, yanking him toward the door.

The three of them bolted for the exit, but before they reached it, the creature moved.

It didn't run—it didn't need to. One moment, it was in the shattered chamber, and the next, it was in front of them, moving with a speed and grace that defied its size.

Jason screamed. Evelyn nearly joined him.

"What the fuck?!" Jason yelled, stumbling back into Malcolm.

"Shut up!" Evelyn hissed, though she had no idea why. It wasn't like the thing couldn't already see them.

The creature tilted its head, studying them like a predator sizing up its prey. Evelyn's heart hammered in her chest as it let out another low growl, deeper and more resonant.

"Don't move," she whispered, knowing it was useless. If this thing wanted to kill them, they were fucked no matter what they did.

Jason, of course, didn't listen. He stepped back, tripping over his feet and crashing into a table of lab equipment. The noise was deafening in the silence.

"Jason, you fucking idiot!" Evelyn snapped.

"I'm sorry!" he hissed, trying to scramble back to his feet.

The creature's head snapped toward him, its body tensing like it was about to pounce. Evelyn's stomach dropped.

"Oh, shit," she whispered. "Jason, don't—"

But it was too late.

The creature lunged, and Jason screamed, throwing his hands up as if that would protect him. Evelyn grabbed the nearest thing she could—a metal rod from the table—and swung it with everything she had.

The rod connected with the creature's side, letting out a high-pitched screech, stumbling back just enough to give Jason time to scramble out of the way.

"Run!" Evelyn shouted, not waiting to see if they listened.

She bolted for the door, her heart pounding so hard it felt like it might burst. Jason and Malcolm were right behind her, both panting and cursing under their breath.

They made it into the corridor, slamming the door shut behind them. Evelyn didn't stop running until they were halfway to the control room.

"Okay," Jason gasped, leaning against the wall. "What the fuck was that?!"

"That," Evelyn said, hands on her knees as she tried to catch her breath, "was what happens when people like Malcolm here decide to play god."

"Don't you dare blame this on me!" Malcolm snapped. "You don't even know what's going on yet!"

"Yeah? Well, here's what I do know: that thing is loose, it's fast as hell, and we're all going to die unless you come up with something better than, 'Let's stand here and argue about it.'"

Jason raised a hand. "Uh, I vote for running and screaming. Preferably screaming away from the murder monster."

Evelyn glared at him. "Your contribution is noted, Jason. Now shut the fuck up and let me think."

Chapter Four

Containment Failure

The sound of the alarms was deafening now, a constant droning wail that felt like it was drilling into Evelyn's skull. Red warning lights strobed through the corridors, casting everything in a hellish glow. It was the kind of cinematic nightmare she'd never imagined being in—except this wasn't a movie, and there wasn't a damn script to follow.

"Okay, okay," Jason panted as they ran, glancing over his shoulder. "Does anyone have an actual plan, or are we just running around waiting to die?"

"Jason, I swear to God—" Evelyn started, but she didn't get to finish because a loud crash echoed behind them.

They all stopped, frozen in place. The crash had come from the door they'd just bolted through—the one they had slammed shut.

"Oh, fuck me," Jason whispered.

Evelyn turned slowly, her stomach doing somersaults. The door was bent inward, the reinforced metal crumpled like tinfoil.

"Great," she muttered, gripping her knees as she caught her breath. "So much for containment."

"Why the hell didn't the lockdown work?" Jason asked, his voice climbing into that high-pitched tone that grated on Evelyn's nerves.

"Because this lab is a piece of shit," she snapped, straightening up. "And because Malcolm probably spent more money on the coffee machines than the goddamn security system."

"I don't even drink coffee!" Malcolm shouted, his voice cracking.

"Well, that's the least of your fucking problems right now, isn't it?" Evelyn shot back.

Another crash interrupted their argument. This time, it wasn't the door—it was the sound of something large and heavy moving through the corridor behind them.

Evelyn's blood ran cold.

"Move," she said, her voice low but urgent. "Now."

They sprinted down the hall, their footsteps echoing off the walls. Evelyn tried to focus on the route ahead, but it was hard when every instinct screamed at her to look back, to see how close it was.

"You know," Jason panted, his words coming out in gasps, "I used to think working in a top-secret lab would be cool. Like, sci-fi movie cool. Turns out, it fucking sucks."

"No one forced you to take the job, Jason," Evelyn snapped, even though a tiny part of her agreed with him.

"I'm pretty sure student loan debt did," he shot back.

"Shut up, both of you!" Malcolm barked. "We need to focus!"

"Oh, now you're the voice of reason?" Evelyn shot him a glare but didn't slow down. "Where was all this focus when we were building monsters?"

"I didn't build it!" Malcolm snapped. "I approved the research! There's a difference!"

"Oh, right, yeah," Jason wheezed. "That makes it so much better. Thanks, Malcolm, I feel so safe now."

Another crash behind them silenced the bickering. Evelyn risked a glance back and wished she hadn't.

The creature was there. It was faster than it had any right to be, its long limbs propelling it forward with an almost insect-like efficiency. The way it moved wasn't natural—it was too smooth, too calculated like it was studying them as it chased them.

"Shit, shit, shit!" Evelyn hissed, forcing her legs to move faster.

"Is it raining on us?" Jason called out, panic in his voice.

"What do you think?!" she snapped, not looking back again.

They skidded around a corner and into a large storage room. Evelyn slammed her hand on the control panel by the door, and the heavy security door began to close. It was slow—too slow—but there was no other choice.

"Come on, come on!" she muttered, watching the gap shrink agonizingly slowly.

Jason and Malcolm dove inside, and Evelyn followed, slamming her palm against the emergency override button. As the creature rounded the corner, the door was sealed with a loud thunk.

For a moment, the only sound was their ragged breathing. Evelyn leaned against the wall, clutching her side.

"Is it... is it gone?" Jason asked, his voice trembling.

"No," Evelyn said flatly. "It's just waiting."

A deep, guttural sound rumbled from the other side of the door as if on cue. It wasn't quite a growl—it was almost... amused.

"Yeah, that's comforting," Jason muttered, sliding down the wall and burying his face in his hands. "It's fucking laughing at us now."

"Well, it's got a better sense of humor than you," Evelyn said, forcing a grin she didn't feel.

"Funny," Jason shot back, his voice muffled.

"Enough," Malcolm said, straightening his tie like that would somehow make him feel in control again. "We need to figure out a plan."

Evelyn gave him a withering look. "A plan? Oh, great, Malcolm's got a plan! Let me guess—it involves throwing a bunch of paperwork at it until it dies of boredom?"

"Do you ever stop talking?" Malcolm snapped.

"Not when I'm trapped in a murder maze with a fucking science experiment gone wrong!" she shot back.

The sound of metal screeching cut through their argument. Evelyn's stomach dropped as she realized what was happening.

"It's trying to get through," she said, her voice tight.

"Through that?" Jason pointed at the heavy door. "It can't get through that. Right?"

Evelyn didn't answer. She didn't want to lie, but she also didn't want to tell him that it absolutely could.

The screeching grew louder, and a new sound joined—a low, rhythmic thud. It was banging against the door, testing it.

Jason's face went pale. "So... anyone wants to bet on how long that door holds?"

"No one is betting, Jason," Evelyn snapped. "We're going to figure this out."

"Oh yeah? What's your brilliant plan, huh?" Jason stood, his voice rising. "Because unless you've got a monster-killing ray gun hidden in here, I'm thinking we're pretty much fucked!"

Evelyn opened her mouth to reply, but before she could, the banging stopped.

The silence was worse.

"Oh no," Jason whispered, looking around wildly. "Why did it stop? What does that mean?"

"It means it's thinking," Evelyn said grimly.

Jason's eyes widened. "It thinks?!"

"Great," Malcolm muttered, pacing. "Now we're dealing with a genius predator. That's just fantastic."

Chapter Five

Survival Instincts

The silence was suffocating. Evelyn could feel her pulse hammering in her ears as the three stood frozen in the storage room, staring at the door. The banging had stopped, but that didn't mean the creature had given up.

Jason broke the silence first, his voice trembling. "I don't know what's worse—the banging or the fact that it's just... standing out there."

"Standing?" Evelyn whispered, her voice dripping with sarcasm. "Oh, sure, Jason, let's assume it's standing there politely waiting to knock again. Maybe it's writing us a fucking apology letter while it's at it."

Jason glared at her, but a sound cut through the tension before he could fire back.

A scrape.

It started low and slow, like claws dragging against the metal door. The noise sent a chill racing up Evelyn's spine.

"Oh, no, no, no," Jason muttered, pacing in frantic circles. "This is some horror movie shit. This is exactly how we die. I mean, come on, listen to that! It's taunting us!"

"Shut up, Jason," Evelyn hissed, her eyes fixed on the door.

"I'm serious!" Jason continued, his voice rising. "That thing out there? It's smarter than us, faster than us, and it's probably thinking about how to peel off our skin and wear it as a suit!"

Evelyn shot him a glare. "Jason, if you don't shut up, I will peel myself."

Malcolm, who had been eerily quiet until now, finally spoke, his tone sharp. "We need to move. This room won't hold. And if it gets in here, we're sitting ducks."

Evelyn snorted. "Great observation, Captain Obvious. Do you have any suggestions on moving without becoming dinner?"

Malcolm's jaw clenched. "There's a backup containment corridor two floors up. It's reinforced. If we can get there, we might be able to trap it."

"'Might,'" Jason repeated bitterly. "Yeah, sure, let's put our lives on a 'might.' That sounds solid."

"It's that or wait here for it to rip us apart," Malcolm snapped.

Jason opened his mouth to argue but shut it again when another sound came from the door. This time, it was different. A low, guttural growl reverberated through the room, sending a wave of primal fear.

"Fuck it," Jason whispered. "Let's run."

Evelyn held her breath as Malcolm unlocked the door. The moment it slid open, the three of them bolted into the hallway, their footsteps echoing like gunshots against the cold, metallic walls.

The red emergency lights strobed, casting the corridor in flickering shadows. Every dark corner felt alive like the creature could leap any second.

"Which way?" Evelyn hissed, glancing over her shoulder.

"Left!" Malcolm barked, pointing down the hall.

They skidded around the corner and sprinted toward the stairwell. The sound of claws scraping against metal filled the air behind them, accompanied by the heavy, rhythmic thuds of something impossibly large giving chase.

"It's right behind us!" Jason screamed, his voice cracking. "Oh my God, it's fucking behind us!"

"No shit!" Evelyn snapped, her lungs burning.

They burst into the stairwell, slamming the door shut behind them. Malcolm jammed a metal bar through the handle, securing it as best he could.

"Move!" he barked, shoving Jason up the stairs.

The stairwell was narrow and steep, the kind of place that made you feel claustrophobic even when you weren't running for your life. Evelyn's legs felt like jelly as she climbed, her ragged breathing drowning out her thoughts.

Then the banging started again.

It was louder and more ferocious this time. The door shook violently as the creature slammed into it repeatedly.

"Fucking hurry!" Evelyn shouted, practically shoving Jason up the steps.

They reached the second floor just as the door below gave way with a deafening crash.

"Oh shit, oh shit, oh shit," Jason muttered, practically tripping over his own feet.

Evelyn looked down the stairwell but then decided against it.

The creature was climbing. Fast.

Its long limbs bent at unnatural angles as it scaled the stairs, its glossy black eyes fixed on her. Its mouth—if you could call it that—stretched open, revealing rows of jagged, needle-like teeth.

"Don't stop!" she screamed, tearing her gaze away and shoving Jason forward.

They rushed into the second-floor hallway, slamming the door shut. Malcolm quickly keyed in the override code for the backup containment corridor.

"Hurry the fuck up!" Evelyn shouted, glancing back at the door.

"I'm going as fast as I can!" Malcolm snapped, his fingers flying across the keypad.

Jason was hyperventilating, his back pressed against the wall. "It's going to kill us. We're dead. We're so fucking dead."

"Jason, shut up!" Evelyn barked; her panic barely held.

The banging started again. This time, it was against the second-floor door.

"I'm almost there!" Malcolm said, his voice frantic.

The door creaked under the force of the creature's blows, the metal already starting to buckle.

"Malcolm!" Evelyn shouted, stepping back from the door.

"I got it!" he yelled as the containment corridor door slid open.

"Go!" Evelyn screamed, shoving Jason inside. She and Malcolm followed, and the door slid shut just as the creature smashed through the second-floor door.

For a moment, there was silence.

Then, the creature slammed into the containment door.

Evelyn backed away, her entire body trembling. Through the reinforced glass, she could see its shadow, its massive frame outlined by the strobing red lights.

"What now?" Jason whispered, his voice barely audible.

Evelyn looked at Malcolm. "You said this place was reinforced. Will it hold?"

Malcolm didn't answer. His silence was enough.

The creature let out a deafening screech and slammed into the door again, harder this time. The glass cracked.

"Oh, fuck me," Jason whispered.

Evelyn grabbed a fire axe from the wall, gripping it tightly. "If that thing gets through, we're not going down without a fight."

Jason stared at her like she was insane. "A fight? With that? Are you kidding me?"

"Got a better idea?" Evelyn snapped, her knuckles white around the axe handle.

Jason opened his mouth to reply, but the sound of shattering glass cut him off.

The creature was inside.

Chapter Six

The Truth

The creature burst through the shattered glass, a nightmarish blur of jagged teeth, glossy black eyes, and too many limbs moving in ways no living thing should. Evelyn's breath hitched as she raised the fire axe, her palms slick with sweat.

"Fuck, fuck, fuck!" Jason screamed, diving behind a metal table.

"Jason!" Evelyn snapped, her voice shaking. "Get your ass up and help me!"

"Help you what?!" he yelled, peeking out from his hiding spot. "That thing is a fucking horror show! You want me to die faster?!"

Evelyn didn't have time to argue. The creature lunged forward, its unnaturally long arms sweeping toward her with terrifying speed. She barely dodged, swinging the axe with all her strength and connecting with one of its limbs.

The axe bit deep, and the creature released a guttural screech reverberating through the containment corridor. Dark, viscous liquid—thicker than blood—spattered across the floor, the walls, and Evelyn's face.

"Oh, Jesus Christ," she muttered, stumbling back and wiping the sludge off her cheek. It smelled like burnt plastic and rot. "What the fuck are you made of?"

The creature hissed, its body convulsing as if the wound only pissed it off more.

"Great," Jason muttered from behind the table. "You made it angry. Fantastic job."

"Oh, I'm sorry. Would you like to take a turn?" Evelyn shouted, gripping the axe tighter.

Before Jason could respond, the creature moved again, faster than Evelyn could react. Its clawed hand lashed out, slamming into her side and sending her flying into the wall. The impact knocked the wind out of her, and she collapsed to the floor, gasping for air.

"Evelyn!" Jason's voice cracked with panic.

Frantically working at the control panel, Malcolm finally shouted, "Get its attention! I need time to activate the emergency purge system!"

Jason gaped at him. "Oh, sure, Malcolm. Let me just wave a fucking flag and invite it to tear me apart! That sounds great!"

Malcolm shot him a glare. "Do you want to live or not?"

Jason groaned, muttering a string of curses under his breath. He grabbed a metal chair and hurled it at the creature.

"Hey, ugly!" he shouted, his voice shaking. "Over here, you slimy piece of shit!"

The chair hit the creature square in the chest, and for a moment, it stopped. Its head tilted toward Jason, its black eyes narrowing as if it was deciding whether he was worth the effort.

"Oh, fuck me," Jason whispered, taking a step back. "Bad idea. Bad idea."

The creature lunged toward him, its claws slicing through the air. Jason let out a high-pitched scream and dove under the table, narrowly avoiding getting skewered.

Meanwhile, Evelyn forced herself to her feet, clutching her ribs. She wasn't sure if they were bruised or broken, but it didn't matter. She grabbed the axe again, her vision blurring from the pain.

"Malcolm, how much longer?" she shouted.

"Almost there!" he yelled, his fingers flying over the control panel.

The creature slammed into the table Jason was hiding under, flipping it effortlessly. Jason scrambled backward, holding his hands like that would somehow stop the monster.

"Oh, shit, oh, shit—Evelyn, do something!"

"Hold still!" she barked, charging forward.

She swung the axe again, aiming for the creature's torso. The blade sank into its side, and the beast released another unholy screech. It whipped around, one of its limbs striking her arm and knocking the axe out of her hands.

"Goddammit!" Evelyn hissed, clutching her arm.

The creature loomed over her, its jaw unhinged to reveal rows of teeth spiraling inward like a black hole. For a split second, she thought this was it—this was how she was going to die.

But then Malcolm shouted, "Got it!"

The lights in the corridor flickered, and a deep, mechanical hum filled the room. Evelyn didn't know what Malcolm had done but didn't care if it worked.

The creature hesitated, its head snapping toward the ceiling as gas began to pour into the room through hidden vents.

"What the hell is that?" Jason shouted, coughing as the gas filled the air.

"Neutralizing agent," Malcolm said, covering his mouth with his sleeve. "It's supposed to incapacitate anything organic."

Jason glared at him. "Including us?"

"Probably not!" Malcolm snapped.

"Probably? Oh, great, that's fucking reassuring!"

The creature let out a guttural roar, its movements becoming frantic as the gas took effect. Its limbs twitched uncontrollably and slammed against the walls, desperately trying to escape.

Evelyn staggered back, coughing and clutching her ribs. She watched as the creature's movements grew slower and more erratic, its guttural roars fading into wet, choking sounds.

Finally, it collapsed, its massive body hitting the floor with a sickening thud.

"Is it... is it dead?" Jason asked, his voice shaking.

Evelyn didn't answer. She stepped forward cautiously, her heart pounding as she stared at the creature's still form.

It wasn't moving.

She exhaled shakily, lowering the fire axe. "Yeah. It's dead."

Malcolm leaned heavily against the wall, sweat dripping down his face. "We need to get out of here before the gas spreads."

"No argument there," Evelyn muttered. She turned to Jason, still sitting on the floor, looking like he might pass out. "Are you coming, or are you just going to live here now?"

Jason blinked at her, then scrambled to his feet. "Yeah, yeah, I'm coming. Jesus, give me a minute. I just had a fucking heart attack."

"Welcome to the club," Evelyn said, wincing as she started toward the exit.

As they left the containment corridor, Evelyn couldn't shake the nagging feeling that something wasn't right. She glanced back at the creature's body one last time, a knot of unease twisting in her gut.

Something about the way it had died didn't sit well with her. It was too... easy.

But she pushed the thought aside. They were alive, and that was all that mattered.

For now.

Chapter Seven

The Final Stand

The quiet in the aftermath was almost worse than the chaos before. The three trudged through the empty corridors, their footsteps echoing against the walls. Red emergency lights continued to pulse, bathing everything in a disorienting glow. Evelyn gripped the fire axe tighter, her hands trembling from the encounter.

"Okay," Jason said, his voice barely above a whisper. "So, uh… what now? Do we… leave? Because I vote for leaving. Like, right fucking now."

"We can't leave," Malcolm snapped, his voice strained. "That thing wasn't just some random anomaly. There's more going on here."

"Oh, for fuck's sake, Malcolm," Evelyn groaned. "Can you save your conspiracy theories for later? Do you want to play detective? Be my guest. But I'm leaving before something else tries to eat me."

Jason nodded furiously. "Yeah, I'm with her. Let's find the nearest exit and run."

"No," Malcolm said firmly, stopping in his tracks. "You don't understand. This isn't over. That thing—it wasn't acting on instinct. It was deliberate. Intelligent. And if there's even a chance something else in this lab is compromised—"

Evelyn turned on him, her eyes blazing. "Compromised? Malcolm, the whole goddamn lab is compromised! Did you miss the part where a fucking monster tried to rip us apart?!"

Malcolm didn't back down. "I'm telling you, there's more to this than you think. And if we don't stop it—if we just run—we might be unleashing something worse."

Jason threw up his hands. "Worse? What's worse than that thing? What, does it have a big brother lurking around somewhere?"

The thought sent a chill down Evelyn's spine, but she refused to let it show. "We'll deal with that if it happens. Right now, staying here just gets us killed."

A loud crash echoed deeper into the lab, cutting off the argument.

"What the fuck was that?" Jason whispered, his eyes darting toward the sound.

Evelyn tightened her grip on the axe. "Guess we're about to find out."

They moved cautiously, their footsteps soft against the floor. The tension in the air was suffocating, and every shadow and sound amplified their fear.

"Malcolm," Evelyn hissed. "Now would be a good time if you've got any brilliant ideas."

He glanced at her, his face pale but determined. "There's a failsafe. A full-lab purge. It'll neutralize everything—pathogens, specimens, all of it."

"Neutralize?" Jason asked, his voice shaking. "What does that mean? Like... blow everything up?"

Malcolm nodded grimly. "Essentially, yes. Total incineration."

Jason stopped walking. "Whoa, whoa, whoa. Blow everything up? Including us?"

"It's a last resort," Malcolm said, his tone clipped. "But if that's what it takes to contain this—"

"Fucking not!" Jason shouted, throwing his hands in the air. "I did not sign up to be vaporized!"

"Shut up!" Evelyn hissed. "Do you want that thing to hear us?"

Jason clamped his mouth shut, but his eyes were wide with panic.

They reached the main server room, where the failsafe could be activated. The door was ajar, and a faint, wet, squelching sound came from inside.

Evelyn froze. "Do you hear that?"

Jason nodded, his face pale. "Yeah. And I hate it."

Malcolm ignored them and stepped toward the door. Evelyn grabbed his arm.

"Are you insane?" she whispered. "We don't know what's in there!"

"We don't have time to wait," he snapped, pulling free.

Before Evelyn could stop him, Malcolm pushed the door open and stepped inside.

The sight that greeted them was nothing short of horrifying.

The creature wasn't dead. It was in the center of the room, its body twitching as it fed on one of the lab techs. The poor bastard's torso was a mess of gore, his arms dangling limply as the creature ripped into him with its jagged teeth.

Jason let out a strangled noise, stumbling back. "Oh my God... oh my fucking God..."

The creature turned its head slowly, its black eyes locking onto them. It let out a low, guttural growl and dropped the body with a sickening thud.

"Run," Evelyn whispered.

The three of them bolted, the creature screeching as it gave chase.

They sprinted down the corridor, but the creature was faster. It leaped onto the walls, its limbs bending at impossible angles as it closed the distance.

Jason tripped, falling hard onto the floor. "Fuck! Help me!"

Evelyn skidded to a stop and turned back, her heart pounding. "Get up, Jason!"

"I can't!" he cried, scrambling to his knees.

The creature lunged at him, its claws raking across his back. Jason let out a bloodcurdling scream as it pinned him to the floor.

"Jason!" Evelyn screamed, raising the axe and charging forward.

She swung the axe into the creature's side, and it screeched in pain, releasing Jason momentarily. Blood—or whatever passed for blood in its veins—spattered across the floor.

"Go!" Evelyn shouted at Jason, who was crawling away, his face contorted in pain.

But the creature recovered too quickly. It grabbed Jason by the leg and yanked him back.

"NO!" Evelyn screamed, swinging the axe again, but the creature batted her away like a rag doll this time. She hit the wall hard; the air was knocked out of her.

Jason's screams were abruptly cut off as the creature's jaws clamped down on his throat.

Evelyn could only watch in horror as Jason's body went limp, his blood pooling beneath him.

"No..." she whispered, tears streaming down her face.

Malcolm grabbed her arm, pulling her to her feet. "We must go. Now."

Evelyn didn't want to leave Jason but knew he was gone.

They ran, the creature too distracted by its kill to follow at once.

When they finally reached the failsafe control room, Evelyn turned to Malcolm, her face grim.

"Activate it," she said.

Malcolm hesitated. "But—"

"Do it!" she screamed, her voice raw.

Malcolm nodded, his hands shaking as he entered the code.

Alarms blared, and a robotic voice announced: "Failsafe activated. Purge sequence starting in five minutes."

Evelyn gripped the fire axe, her knuckles white. "Let's make sure it doesn't leave this lab alive."

The creature's screech echoed through the corridors, growing louder as it approached.

The final stand was about to begin.

Chapter Eight

Fallout

The alarms blared through the facility, a robotic voice counting to oblivion.

"Purge sequence commencing in T-minus four minutes."

Evelyn wiped the blood from her face, her breaths ragged and uneven. The fire axe felt heavier in her hands now, Jason's screams still fresh in her ears. Malcolm was typing furiously at the failsafe console, pale but resolute.

"Four minutes isn't enough," he muttered, his voice barely audible over the chaos. "We need more time to contain this."

"We don't have more time!" Evelyn shouted, her voice breaking. "You saw what it did to Jason! If that thing gets out—"

"It's not getting out!" Malcolm snapped, slamming his fist against the console. "I've locked down every exit. The purge will kill everything in this lab, including us."

Evelyn froze. "What do you mean, including us?"

Malcolm turned to her, his eyes grim. "There's no time to override the sequence. We're not making it out of here."

Evelyn's stomach sank. She stared at him, her mind racing. "You knew this was a suicide mission?"

He didn't answer. That was all she needed.

"You son of a bitch," she whispered. "You fucking knew."

Before Malcolm could respond, a loud screech tore through the air. The creature was coming; this time, it wouldn't stop until they were dead.

Evelyn gripped the axe tighter, her knuckles white. "Get ready."

The door to the control room exploded inward, torn apart like it was made of paper. The creature lunged inside, its jagged teeth bared, its black eyes gleaming with a terrifying intelligence.

"Malcolm, MOVE!" Evelyn screamed, shoving him aside as the creature charged.

It swiped at her with one of its elongated claws, and she ducked just in time. The force of the swing sent sparks flying as it struck the wall behind her. She swung the axe in return, the blade biting deep into the creature's shoulder.

It howled, a deafening, guttural sound that shook the entire room. Black sludge oozed from the wound, hissing as it hit the floor.

"Evelyn, over here!" Malcolm shouted, holding a fire extinguisher.

She didn't have time to argue. Malcolm hurled the extinguisher at the creature's face, the impact stunning it for just a moment.

"Go for the head!" he yelled, grabbing a metal rod and charging at the monster.

"Malcolm, no!" Evelyn screamed, but it was too late.

Malcolm swung the rod with all his might, slamming it into the creature's head. It barely flinched.

Instead, it turned to him, letting out a low, guttural growl.

"Shit," Malcolm whispered, realizing his mistake.

The creature lunged, its claws tearing through his chest like butter. Blood sprayed across the room as Malcolm let out a choked scream, collapsing to the floor.

"NO!" Evelyn screamed, tears streaming down her face.

The creature didn't stop. It sank its jagged teeth into Malcolm's throat, ripping and tearing until the gurgling stopped. His lifeless body hit the floor with a sickening thud.

Evelyn stumbled back, her heart racing. She was alone now. It was just her and the monster.

"Come on, you fucker," she muttered, gripping the axe tighter. "Let's finish this."

The creature turned to her, its glossy black eyes narrowing. It lunged again, and Evelyn swung the axe with everything she had, catching it in the side of the neck.

The blade sank deep, and the creature screeched, its movements jerky and frantic. Evelyn yanked the axe free and swung again, aiming for its head.

The blade connected with a sickening crunch, splitting its skull. Black sludge poured from the wound, pooling around its feet.

But it didn't stop.

The creature swiped at her, its claws raking across her shoulder. Evelyn screamed, stumbling back and clutching the wound. Blood seeped through her fingers, but she refused to give up.

"Die already!" she screamed, swinging the axe one last time.

This time, the blade cleaved through its neck, severing its head from its body. The creature collapsed to the floor, its limbs twitching before finally going still.

"Purge sequence commencing in T-minus one minute."

Evelyn dropped the axe, her entire body trembling. The creature was dead, but the lab was seconds away from being incinerated.

She staggered to the console, her vision blurring from blood loss. Malcolm's body lay crumpled on the floor beside her, his lifeless eyes staring at nothing.

"I'm not dying here," she muttered, slamming her hands on the keyboard. "Come on, come on..."

Her fingers flew over the keys, bypassing security protocols and inputting the override code Malcolm had shown her earlier.

Thirty seconds.

The console beeped. The purge sequence paused.

Evelyn let out a shaky breath, tears streaming down her face. She'd done it.

But she wasn't safe yet.

She stumbled through the corridors, her vision fading in and out. The lab was a war zone, with blood and debris everywhere. The smell of death clung to her like a second skin.

Finally, she reached the main exit. The lockdown had been lifted.

She shoved the door open and stepped into the night, the chilly air biting her skin. The storm had passed, leaving the sky eerily clear.

Evelyn collapsed onto the grass, staring up at the stars.

She was alive.

But the memories of what she'd seen, what she'd done, would haunt her forever.

The final scene: Evelyn sits in the back of an ambulance, wrapped in a blanket. She stares at the smoking remains of the lab in the distance, her expression unreadable.

"Dr. Harper," a paramedic says, his voice hesitant. "Is there... is there anything you need?"

She doesn't respond at first. Then she looks at him, her eyes hollow.

"Burn it all," she whispers.

The paramedic frowns. "It's already gone, ma'am."

Evelyn doesn't answer. She knows better. She knows the creature wasn't the only thing the lab was hiding.

And she knows it's not over.

Epilogue

Echoes of the Lab

Evelyn sat alone in her small apartment, the only sound the faint hum of the refrigerator in the kitchen. A glass of whiskey sat untouched on the table in front of her, the amber liquid catching the dim light of the room. She hadn't slept since the night she escaped the lab. Not really. Every time she closed her eyes, she saw Jason's face, heard Malcolm's screams, and smelled the rancid stench of the creature's blood.

It had been two weeks since the lab burned to the ground, reduced to ash by the failsafe. Officially, the facility's destruction was attributed to a "chemical fire." That's what the news had reported—an accident—a tragedy.

She knew better.

Her phone buzzed on the table, making her flinch. She stared at it momentarily, her heart pounding, before finally picking it up. It was an unknown number. She almost let it go to voicemail, but something compelled her to answer.

"Hello?" she said, her voice hoarse.

"Dr. Harper," a man's voice said on the other end. It was calm, professional, and laced with something cold and calculating. "We need to talk."

Her blood ran cold. "Who is this?"

"That's not important," the man replied. "What is important is the data you copied before the purge."

Evelyn's grip on the phone tightened. She glanced at the flash drive on the table beside her glass of whiskey—the one she had grabbed in the chaos, almost without thinking. She hadn't dared to open the files yet. Some part of her didn't want to know what was on it.

"I don't know what you're talking about," she said, trying to keep her voice steady.

"You're lying, Dr. Harper," the man said, his tone devoid of emotion. "And you're not very good at it."

Evelyn's pulse quickened. "If you know so much, you know what happened in that lab. You know what I saw. You know why I destroyed it."

There was a long pause on the other end of the line. Then the man said, "What you destroyed was one facility. One project. But it wasn't the only one."

Evelyn's stomach churned. "What do you mean?"

"Specimen X wasn't unique," the man said. "It was part of a larger program. And you, Dr. Harper, are now the only person who can stop it."

She felt like the air had been sucked out of the room. "No," she whispered. "You're lying. That thing was a mistake. An experiment gone wrong."

The man's tone didn't change. "You're naïve if you think that was the end. The files on that drive will tell you everything. You can choose to ignore them, of course. But I don't think you will."

Evelyn's hand trembled as she looked at the flash drive again. She wanted to throw it out the window, to smash it into pieces and forget it existed. But she knew she wouldn't.

"Why me?" she asked, her voice barely audible.

"Because you survived," the man said simply. "And because you know what's at stake."

The line went dead.

Evelyn glanced at the phone and then back at the flash drive. She wanted to walk away but knew she had to face the truth.

She couldn't.

With a deep breath, she picked up the flash drive and plugged it into her laptop. The screen lit up, lines of encrypted data scrolling across the monitor. As she decrypted the first file, a single thought echoed in her mind:

It's not over.

Afterword

When I first began writing the stories in *Fragments of Fear*, I never imagined they would come together as my debut collection. Each tale began as a spark—sometimes a single image, a question, or even a quiet thought that refused to let go. Piece by piece, those sparks grew into the worlds you've just walked through.

This book is more than a collection of stories. It is a milestone, a reminder that even in the middle of long days, late nights, and countless doubts, creativity can't be silenced. Fear is universal—it touches all of us in different ways— and through these pages, I wanted to explore how it shapes, twists, and reveals who we really are.

If you felt unsettled, if you found yourself questioning shadows, or if even one story stayed with you longer than expected, then this book has done its job.

Thank you for taking this journey with me, for letting my words creep into your imagination. This is only the beginning. More stories are waiting, and I invite you to step into them with me—one twist, one shiver, on fragment of fear at a time.

— R. Rivera

About the author

R. Rivera writes stories that linger in the dark corners of the mind. His debut collection, *Fragments of Fear*, brings together chilling tales of suspense, each designed to leave readers unsettled long after the final page.

Raised in Texas, Rivera grew up with a fascination for what lies beneath the ordinary—the whispers in empty rooms, the storm that rattles more than just windows, the secrets people try to bury. That fascination grew into a love of storytelling, where imagination meets unease.

When not writing, Rivera can be found exploring new places, enjoying puzzles and games, or traveling the open seas on his yearly cruise. His goal is simple: to craft stories that make readers feel—whether through fear, tension, or an unexpected twist that changes everything.

www.ingramcontent.com/pod-product-compliance
Lightning Source LLC
LaVergne TN
LVHW010600100826
845148LV00014B/2781

* 9 7 9 8 2 1 8 7 8 6 0 3 8 *